# AFTER THE END HAS BEGUN

CIA ROSE BOOK TWO

## RICK WOOD

BLOOD SPLATTER PRESS

# ABOUT THE AUTHOR

Rick Wood is a British writer born in Cheltenham.

His love for writing came at an early age, as did his battle with mental health. After defeating his demons, he grew up and became a stand-up comedian, then a drama and English teacher, before giving it all up to become a full-time author.

He now lives in Loughborough, where he divides his time between watching horror, reading horror, and writing horror.

**The Sensitives:**

*Book One – The Sensitives*

*Book Two – My Exorcism Killed Me*

*Book Three – Close to Death*

*Book Four – Demon's Daughter*

*Book Five – Questions for the Devil*

*Book Six - Repent*

*Book Seven - The Resurgence*

*Book Eight - Until the End*

**Shutter House**

*Shutter House*

*Prequel Book One - This Book is Full of Bodies*

**Cia Rose:**

*Book One – After the Devil Has Won*

*Book Two – After the End Has Begun*

*Book Three - After the Living Have Lost*

**Chronicles of the Infected**

*Book One – Zombie Attack*

*Book Two – Zombie Defence*

*Book Three – Zombie World*

**Standalones:**

*When Liberty Dies*

*I Do Not Belong*

*Death of the Honeymoon*

**Sean Mallon:**

*Book One – The Art of Murder*

*Book Two – Redemption of the Hopeless*

**The Edward King Series:**

*Book One – I Have the Sight*

*Book Two – Descendant of Hell*

*Book Three – An Exorcist Possessed*

*Book Four – Blood of Hope*

*Book Five – The World Ends Tonight*

**Non-Fiction**

How to Write an Awesome Novel

*Thrillers published as Ed Grace:*

**The Jay Sullivan Thriller Series**

Assassin Down

Kill Them Quickly

The Bars That Hold Me

# THE MONSTERS

# MASKETES

MASKETES ARE large flying monsters with long snouts, veiny wings, sharp fangs and curved, deadly claws. Large enough that you will see them from a distance, but fast enough that it won't make a difference – they are the true monsters of the sky.

Their diving precision makes them a particularly threatening predator. Once they see their prey on the ground, they dive upon them with such accuracy of aim and expert speed that the fleeing prey can do little about it.

When they do catch their prey, their claws dig deep enough into their food's body so their food doesn't squirm.

Not that they need to pick up their prey if they don't want to – their jaws are sharp enough that they could slice your head clean off on impact.

# THORALS

THESE FOUR-LEGGED, sturdy creatures are good hunters and quick to pounce – but their most terrifying feature is their appearance. Overwhelming in size, with red eyes and jaws that salivate the blood of their victims.

Their only weakness is that you can hear them coming from miles away – such is the earth-shaking thud that announces their presence.

Their sense of smell and hearing means they can detect prey from far off. Their teeth are curved and sharp and can slice through the thickest and toughest of meat.

# LISKERS

THE SCARIEST, most vile of all the creatures that crawled out
the earth. They have long, snake-like bodies, thicker than an
aged tree trunk and almost 5 acres long. These bodies are not
only huge, but are coarse and rough; likely to draw blood
should you scrape your skin against them.

These creatures are rare – but for those few that do
encounter them, they are deadly. Their fangs drip poison that
paralyses their victim, meaning their food remains immobile
as they devour it.

# WASTERS

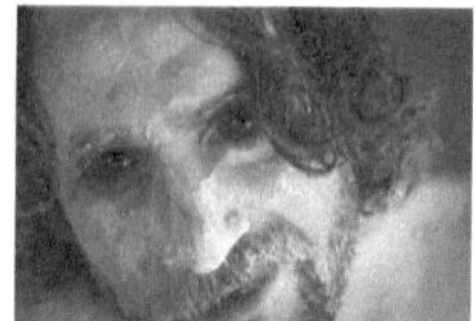

THEY ARE NOT STRICTLY monsters like Masketes, Thorals and Liskers, having been human once – but you should not underestimate these lethal hunters.

These are survivors of the apocalypse who took the coward's way out – choosing to become slaves to the creatures in return for their survival. As part of the deal, they also lost their consciousness, becoming mindless hunters and obedient servants.

Wasters rely on their cannibalistic appetites to survive – and once they spot the person they wish to consume, they will hunt as a pack to intimidate and catch their victim.

Not only to they have a desire to eat human flesh, they have a feral sexual appetite – meaning their victims will often suffer a horrific fate before they are eaten alive.

# THEN

(1 hour after the destruction of the Sanctity)

# CHAPTER ONE

It was done.

Cia could no longer turn back.

Her lethal decision could not be reversed.

She held Boy's hand as they ran, clutched it, refusing to let him go. She had fought through hell to get him back, and she was never letting him out of her sight again.

Dalton kept up with them – Dalton, the man who had gone back to rescue her.

Dalton, the man who'd always had a bed and a roof to return to in the Sanctity.

The Sanctity had been a giant, underground bunker created by the rich to survive the apocalypse. Dalton had been lucky enough to be a soldier the rich were willing to let protect them.

Now the Sanctity was gone. As was Dalton's bed, his friends, and the life he knew – and she was all he had left.

A girl he'd known for days – yet had risked his life to go back and rescue.

*As if I ever need rescuing,* Cia thought with a scoff.

She had done horrific things to survive in this world. Things Dalton would never believe.

You see, Cia was not like Dalton. She and Boy had never had an underground bunker to protect them from the treacherous world they had found themselves in.

They had lived together in the open for all these years – ever since those monsters rose from the ground.

Doing whatever it took to survive.

Hiding from noises.

Relying on luck.

Although, it wasn't always like this. Once upon a time, far before she ever met Boy, Cia and her father had travelled to the Sanctity together; knowing that they both had a place inside. Knowing they would be safe.

Except, there hadn't been room for both of them.

Just her father – the great Doctor Daniel Rose.

*And what a great man he turned out to be...*

He was the man who loved her most.

And yet, he was the man who abandoned her without looking back.

She was left outside to fend for herself, whilst he entered the Sanctity. He had done enough to ensure that he alone survived, and Cia had been too young to understand.

She was a poor girl.

A motherless girl.

*A mixed-race girl.*

And so they would not let her in.

And that was why, when returning to the Sanctity all these years later, she had her revenge.

They'd kept monsters on the ground floor. Bound, drugged, sedated. The subject of experiments.

She'd set them all free.

She'd let the Sanctity find out what it was like to suffer the fate they had forced *her* to suffer.

Dalton didn't know.

Brave, noble Dalton.

Perfect, spotless, youthful, handsome Dalton.

The man who did what was right.

He had gone back to save her, thinking she was a victim like everyone else. Now here he was, with her and Boy, forming a team.

She wanted him to stay. She just didn't know if he would protect her when things were bad – as in, when things were *really* bad.

Most importantly – *would he protect Boy?*

Or would he put the most important thing in the world to her at risk?

Did he even know Boy was autistic? That Boy came with challenges? Would he change his mind if he did?

They ran together, ahead of the few stragglers who'd made it out alive – ahead of all of them except for one.

Cia heard the footsteps before Dalton did. Heavy boots, splashing mud and snapping twigs. Approaching, gaining, with aggression in every step and grunt.

Dalton remained oblivious, and this made her wonder what good he'd be without the instincts she had.

A gun shot.

She, Boy and Dalton stopped and ducked.

They looked up to find a man, standing, feet away from Cia, edging closer and closer until she was in his shadow.

He wore army gear. He was pale-faced. Bags under his eyes. His gun was trembling. His legs were wobbling. He was unstable in his stance and in his mind.

"You..." he grumbled.

*He knows. He knows I did it.*

Was this when Dalton would find out?

They had just begun their life together and here this guy was, ready to end it.

Was this when Dalton would discover that she was the reason all those sick, privileged bastards died?

"I saw you..." the man said, his voice quivering. "I saw what you did..."

She glanced back at Dalton, who was rising to his knees.

"Neil," Dalton said. "Neil, listen to me."

"Shut up, Dalton."

"Neil–"

"I said go to hell!"

The soldier – Neil, apparently – cocked his gun. Directed it at Cia's temple.

"Neil, put the gun down. We're all just trying to survive."

"Survive?"

"Enough people have died today. You're just angry, you're losing it. Think about what you're doing."

"My God..." Neil gasped. "You don't know, do you? Who she is... What she's done..."

Dalton looked at Cia.

Beautiful Cia.

Innocent Cia.

*Terrified* Cia.

"I don't care what she's done," Dalton decided.

So noble. So forthright. So smitten.

*Oh, you do care...* Cia thought. *If only you knew, you'd care... You would care so much...*

"You don't care?" Neil echoed. "You don't even know who she is!"

*Please, Dalton, please don't find out who I am... I want to love you, I want to know you, we can't start out like this, we can't...*

Neil held his gun with a firm grip, taking aim, stroking the trigger.

Cia closed her eyes.

A gunshot fired.

The birds in the nearby tree hastily flew away.

Cia opened her eyes.

Neil was on the floor, squirming and wriggling, his arm bleeding profusely. Dalton was standing behind Cia, his gun still in position, distraught at the sight of what he'd done.

Boy was curled into a ball, covering his ears, closing his eyes, hiding himself away.

Neil tried to lift his wounded arm, tried to direct the gun at Cia. But he couldn't lift the gun fully – meaning the gun was directed at Boy.

His finger feebly stroked the trigger.

She didn't hesitate. She stood, took Neil's gun from his bleeding hand, and put a hole in his head.

And she watched.

Watched as the stranger's eyes emptied and there was no way he could hurt Boy.

Watched as a man died.

She dropped to her knees. Tried to numb her thoughts, to numb the image, to numb the action she had just taken.

She turned and looked at Dalton. Looked for his reaction. Looked to see if this upset him.

To see if he would still want her now.

He said nothing. His face was empty.

He simply held out a hand, and waited for her to take it.

"Come on," he said. "The gunshots may have attracted something, we need to go."

"But, Dalton, I–"

*I'm the one responsible for monsters being loose in the Sanctity.*

*I'm the one who's responsible for the death of all your*

*friends.*

*I'm the one you should hate, should shoot – not Neil, not him.*

"Dalton, he was saying I'm a bad person because–"

"I don't care," Dalton asserted. "I don't care what he had to say. I'll make up my own mind who you are."

"But I–"

"He was going to kill us. We both did what we had to do."

His hand remained, poised, held out for her.

She had to make a decision.

Take that hand and lie to him.

Or bat it away and tell the truth.

His kind eyes looked down on her. His sweet eyes, his eyes that were making her melt. He could take care of Boy with her. He could be everything to her, and she could be everything to him.

And most of all, he could reduce the burden.

Lighten the loneliness.

*He shot Neil... He shot his friend in the arm, to save us...*

He did what he had to.

Maybe he could protect her and Boy.

Maybe he was not a risk. He could be an asset.

*But he doesn't know...*

She had to make a decision.

"Come on," he urged her.

She took his hand and he lifted her up.

He crouched by Boy, took Boy's hands away from his ears, and spoke to him softly.

"Hey, it's time to go now. Okay?"

She watched him help Boy up.

Watched him care for Boy.

Watched him protect Boy.

And she decided she would keep her mouth shut.

NOW

(Six months after the destruction of the Sanctity)

# CHAPTER TWO

Secrets are like a nasty bout of food poisoning.

You must have the food just as you must have the secret –
but it makes you sick, makes you ill, makes you lurch until
your insides have emptied.

Cia knew that she should always keep this secret hidden
away, concealed inside the fortress she built around it. Kept
squashed into a corner, a box constructed with bricks, always
there but within reach.

Sometimes she wondered, considered whether the burden
of knowledge was too heavy, whether her legs would buckle
under its weight, whether she would tire from carrying it
around day after day, after day, after day.

But what was the alternative?

Tell Dalton that she was responsible for the death of
everyone he knew?

Cia had let her resentment get the better of her. She had
been completely taken over by her hatred for that
underground bunker, that *Sanctity*, home to the elitist, rich,
upper-class sycophants who, back when the creatures had
risen, had denied entry to a poor mixed-race girl called Cia

Rose – leaving her, barely an adolescent, to fend for herself in a world full of monsters.

Even now, this far into the future, she was still angry.

*They had deserved it.*

She had watched as the Sanctity collapsed and they were all forced to confront the world they had made her confront, many years ago.

And now she watched Dalton.

Dalton, who had been a soldier in the Sanctity, but was unlike the others – *because he went back for me.*

She watched him, sitting with Boy.

Boy, who Cia had been through hell for.

Boy, who Cia loved enough to kill for – as she had been forced to do.

Boy, who would know nothing of what Cia had done but would always be sure of her love.

It was nice be able to share the burden of looking after Boy with Dalton. Before, it had just been Cia, and she hadn't minded – but now she could sit back, like she was at that moment, and watch as Dalton played with Boy via a stained chess set with three missing pieces they had found when they'd looted an Oxfam store a few weeks ago.

On the board was a balled-up leaf, a stone, and a piece of bark from a nearby tree, replacing the absent queen, knight and pawn.

The chess board had been Dalton's idea. Cia would never have thought of it, but Dalton had clearly said, "It will help him with his...y'know."

*Y'know*, of course, meaning Boy's autism. Something that meant Boy came with extra difficulties – not that Cia had ever considered them difficulties whatsoever. Not once had she felt burdened, or been angry at Boy for panicking at sounds, for covering his ears and screaming when a monster attacked, or for having to recite their special poem when his anxiety became too overwhelming.

She had never even considered it to be an issue.

But she was worried Dalton wouldn't feel the same.

Yet, here he was, playing chess. Dalton had taken on more than his share of responsibilities when it came to Boy. He had done his best to find ways to satisfy Boy's mind, to keep Boy's very active thoughts controlled and stimulated.

Boy made a move and Dalton playfully threw his arms into the air.

"Oh, you got me!" Dalton said. "Damn, you beat me again."

Cia couldn't tell whether Dalton was letting Boy win, or whether Dalton was just that bad.

Boy turned his beaming smile to Cia, so proud of his victory.

"Well done," Cia said, returning his grin. "Looks like you're way better than Dalton."

Dalton shrugged as he stood with a little chuckle.

"What can I say?" Dalton said. "Boy's got skills."

Boy ran up to Cia, throwing his arms around her. Despite Boy being just twelve years old, and her recently turning eighteen (her birthday was normally during the winter, so she was sure they would have passed it seeing as it was now spring), Boy still towered over her.

She was quite petite, mind, and most people did tower over her.

Dalton stretched his muscles and put his hefty bag on his back.

Cia and Dalton's eyes met for a moment. Something unsaid was passed between them like so many times before, but Cia was never sure what it was.

A noise echoed in the distance, possibly a Thoral.

"I think that's our cue," Dalton decided. "We should make a move."

Cia nodded and turned to Boy.

"Do you want to pack up your stuff?"

Boy placed the chess board in his bag, zipped it up, and placed it over his shoulders.

Cia looked at her two boys, at the family she had found, the home she had created without need for a house.

"Ready?" Dalton prompted.

Was she ready?

*Poor Dalton.* He had no idea what she had done to his previous home. No idea what she was responsible for, why all of his friends were dead.

And, looking at the life she had found, she decided he was happier this way. That a life in the open with her was far better than an eternity trapped underground.

"Yep, I'm ready," she answered, and they walked on as she wondered...

How long can a perfect life stay perfect?

# CHAPTER THREE

Dalton was glad that winter was over. Spring had arrived and it was still chilly, but not dangerously so. He hadn't worried about his own warmth; being in the army had forced him to brace himself for treacherous conditions – but he had feared for Cia, and he feared for Boy.

Mostly Boy.

Cia could handle anything. That's why he was so drawn to her.

There was never any hesitance; just alertness.

Never any trepidation; just vigilance.

He was sure she was scared, but she didn't let it rule her – she was a survivor, and a survivor isn't someone that lives without fear; it is someone who is victorious over that fear. They quell it and channel their adrenaline into staying alive.

What's more, at no point had he ever felt wary about involving himself in Boy's life; Cia's caring for Boy was too infectious. From the devotion she showed the child, to never caring about the difficulties he came with. Although, if Dalton was honest with himself, when creatures attacked and Boy shut down, shouting and putting his hands over his ears, he did get worried; it was time they could be running, but were instead having to encourage Boy to move.

But Cia...

She never faltered.

Not once.

She would not leave without Boy.

She'd crouch before him, her voice as calm as if she was reciting directions, her smile warm and her skin gently touching Boy's hands. She would whisper to him, talk him out of it, and they would move.

If it was Dalton, he'd probably panic and shout at Boy to get going. Which, inevitably, would only make it worse.

But not Cia.

No, not Cia.

Maybe she thought Dalton was the one taking care of her, taking care of Boy; she couldn't be more wrong.

She was the one keeping them alive. She had been his motivation to go on after the horrific ordeal at the Sanctity.

After everything they'd witnessed.

*After how everyone had...*

He bowed his head. Winced. Shook himself out of it.

He didn't want to think about it.

He turned his gaze to Cia, who was talking to Boy about all the different trees. Boy could recite their type, estimate their age, and do that crazy thing he did where he would know a hundred facts about a hundred things whilst Dalton could barely remember what he had for breakfast.

That was what he wanted to be thinking about – Cia and Boy.

But the images remained.

*My friends.*

The guys he had lunch with, joked with, circled the

perimeter of the Sanctity with – the guys he'd spent the best part of four years with.

He'd stepped over their faces, their open eyes still staring up at him with nothing behind them. Their bodies pale and empty. Their mouths open, their skin crusted with blood, their insides on the outside and their entrails leaving a bloody pool behind them.

He could never rid his mind of that image.

"Hey, Cia," he said, quelling the thought. "How about lunch soon?"

Cia looked around, listening for noises, placing her fingers on the ground. It was as if she could feel things he couldn't – she would just know if somewhere was safe, and he trusted that.

"Yeah," she answered.

The problem with these images of his friends; the problem with the violence he'd left; was that he'd never understood *why*.

There were many, many bodies, but why?

He wanted to know.

No.

He *needed* to know.

But he didn't want Cia to know that. He didn't want her to know how much this was still hurting him, how little he slept, how much the memories still haunted his nightmares.

"Hey," he called.

"What's up?" she asked. Smiling. That same smile that made his heart beat just that little bit faster.

"I was thinking that, maybe, it would be a good idea to go back to the Sanctity."

For a moment, she said nothing – then followed her silence with, "Are you being serious?"

"Hear me out," he said. "Everyone left in such a hurry.

Everything was abandoned. Think of the supplies that are still there. They could feed us for months."

Her expression morphed between various objections. He could already hear her protests without her needing to open her mouth.

"I mean, you don't have to go in if you don't want," Dalton offered. "You and Boy could wait outside. I could go in and see what there is."

"I wouldn't let you do that."

"I would be fine."

"But what if there was something still in there?"

Dalton shrugged.

"I could take it."

Cia looked back at him, saying nothing, but thinking everything.

Boy stopped by a bush covered in berries. With a nervous smile back at Dalton, she began picking them. She did so with such haste that it made him wonder whether she was that hungry, or whether her speed was as a result of frustration; a convenient diversion from their conversation.

She went to take the first bite of the few she'd gathered for herself, then heard Boy's stomach rumble so loud she thought a Thoral was approaching. Seeing that he had no berries left, she offered hers to him.

Boy shook his head.

"It's fine. My belly's not feeling great, I'm not all that hungry anyway," she lied.

He took the berries and rushed to the shelter of a tree, where he sat and feasted.

"Boy needs more food, too," Dalton said. "We all do. We can't just survive on the berries you pick, or the dirty water in the lake. There will be lots of food left in the Sanctity."

"How would we carry it all?"

"Our bags can hold a lot. We can put smaller stuff in there, like cans."

Cia bowed her head. He knew she didn't want to, but he'd made a compelling argument and they had little choice.

*He* had little choice.

He had to know.

"Like I said, you and Boy can wait outside, or on the top floor. You don't have to come in with me."

"Fine," she answered. "Fine, but we're not waiting on the top floor. We stick together. Right?"

"Okay," he answered.

She smiled that damn smile again.

She looked over at Boy, whose eyes were beginning to shut.

"I guess we're stopping here," Cia said with a chuckle.

Dalton nodded, removed his bag, and began further checks for nearby creatures.

A large burden fell away in a grand sigh. He hadn't realised how much tension he'd been carrying over this, and it felt like a relief to finally know he would soon have the answers.

Finally, he could put those memories to rest, and he could just be happy, with Cia, with Boy, with their new life.

*Our new life.*

If he had only known at the time how destructive those answers would be to that *new life* – he would have never returned to the Sanctity...

# CHAPTER FOUR

Boy's MIND was what Cia loved most about him – how he could gather all the odd bits of information others would most likely discard, and recall them perfectly.

She watched in awe as he ran up to another tree, announcing it this was a wych elm.

"Broadleaf," Boy muttered, inspecting closely. "Toothed leaves, larger than other elms. An asymmetrical base."

Dalton had found a book on trees when they looted a book store a month or so ago and given it to Boy. Boy was now able to identify the trees and recite facts about them with an accuracy Cia assumed was correct – not that she'd know.

Boy rushed to another tree with acorns scattered around its base and pulled a branch down to look at the leaves. He spoke to himself as he studied them: "lobed, these leaves are lobed, rounded or pointed."

He reached his hand out and touched the bark of the tree trunk.

"Small. Scaly. Acorns. This is an oak tree."

It was amazing, the things Boy's brain could do.

She wondered if it was actually the rest of the world that

had the problem, not Boy; especially when Boy's mental abilities were so advanced.

She meandered over to Dalton, who knelt over a tree trunk that had collapsed across their path. He was using his knife to carve something out of it.

"What is that?" Cia asked, looking at its curved shape and wondering what he was up to.

Dalton scraped a few more carvings then lifted an arched piece of wood in the air.

"It is – or, at least, it will be – a bow."

"A bow?"

"Yes."

"And you can just make that out of a tree?"

"Not just any tree. Pine and willow, for example, would be awful – it's best to use oak, like this trunk, or maple or hickory if possible. Now I just need some kind of cord."

"Where are you going to get that from?"

"Don't know. If I could find, like, an unused parachute maybe, or string from a hood. You then tie it here," he indicated a position at the top of the arch, "and here," he indicated a position at the base. "Then make a bunch of sharp points out of more wood for the arrows. I could do with a sander though."

Cia sat down next to him, lifting the arch waiting for the bow, and twisting it beneath her ogling eyes.

"This is incredible," she gasped. "How on earth did you do this?"

Dalton grinned.

"Here, let me show you have to create a bokken."

"A bokken?"

"Yes, it's like a wooden samurai sword. It's a Japanese weapon. Not quite as effective as a blade, but hit it hard enough or create a sharp enough point, and it will do some damage."

Cia watched on eagerly. She'd considered herself resourceful, but she'd never seen weapons so easily crafted out of a discarded tree trunk.

Dalton used his knife to cut out another chunk of wood from the trunk. He carved it, using his thumb to help him guess an inch for the bokken's thickness, and one of his steps at a guess for its four-foot length. He carved out a curve that began from halfway up, and rounded harder at the end, where he also created a sharp point.

He handed the bokken to Cia. It felt rough, splintering her, but she knew that was just because it hadn't been sanded down yet. She turned it over, rotating it, marvelling at what he had done with so little.

"This is incredible," she said.

"Well, now you know if you're ever in a tight spot and weaponless, you can create one like that." He clicked his fingers.

"The handle is rough, but–"

"It's called a tsuka."

"A what?"

"The handle of a Japanese bokken, it's called a tsuka."

"A tsuka..." She mulled the word over, chewing it like a piece of gum.

"And the tip is called a kissaki. The Japanese wouldn't make it so sharp, but that's where I adapted it."

She placed a finger on the tip and felt it prick. Withdrawing her hand she saw a small splodge of blood creeping out of the tip of her finger.

"I told you it was sharp," Dalton said, playfully placing his hands on his hips. "Maybe I should take it back."

He took the bokken and discarded it, throwing it into the bushes.

"Aren't we going to take it?"

"No, I can make better than that," Dalton said. "And we won't have room to carry it after the Sanctity. Besides, there will be far better weapons there."

She looked to Boy, whose mouth was covered in berry juice.

"How long have we got?"

"About twelve miles." He looked to the sky, where the sun was sinking. "It's probably best we get there before dark."

Twelve miles.

Cia's stomach turned suddenly queasy, and she began to wonder why she'd agreed to this.

THEN

# CHAPTER FIVE

DESPITE BEING a grown man in a cafeteria serving fancier food than he knew what to do with, something about the environment always made Dalton feel like he was back at school. Maybe it was the rows of tables, or the plastic trays, or the process of collecting your food then searching for a table where some of your friends are. No matter how much one grows up, there's always some kind of aversion to sitting alone in the cafeteria, as if it means you aren't one of the cool kids.

As it was, Dalton saw Brooklyn sat amongst another group of soldiers with a space saved for him. Dalton made his way over, wondering what it was Brooklyn had said that had made all the other guys crack up.

"Hey man," Brooklyn said. "How's it going?"

"All right," Dalton answered. That's the thing about living in an oversized underground bunker – there wasn't really much to 'tell' about your day.

"You out this afternoon?"

"Nah, tomorrow. Just a perimeter walk I reckon."

"Ah, sweet, think I'm with you."

From across the cafeteria, Dalton spotted her. The same

woman he'd spotted every lunch time. Pretty, long hair, slim. The kind of woman every other guy was looking at.

Another thing about living in an oversized underground bunker – you know most people by face. And another thing – you go slightly crazy. Dalton had practically given this woman a whole backstory despite never having spoken to her. She was once a librarian, now she looked after the documents that preserve human history. She once had three cats, loved to read romantic thrillers, and had a boyfriend called Mike that used to drive a Ferrari and unfortunately perished like most did when the creatures rose. Specifically, he was killed by a Thoral, and Dalton always took a bit of satisfaction in picturing this imaginary boyfriend being ripped apart, some kind of jealousy for a fictional scenario about a woman he didn't even know.

"Why don't you go talk to her?" Brooklyn asked.

Dalton shrugged.

"What's the worst that could happen?"

"She could talk back," Dalton joked between mouthfuls of bread. "Problem is, if you hit on someone here, and they reject you, then you have to look at each other every day from then on. Even worse; if they don't reject you, but date you then dump you, then you're stuck in here with your ex."

"As if that's the reason." Brooklyn winked.

"Nah, it's 'cause he's chickenshit," interjected Eric Piper, the resident dickhead. The kind of guy that hung around with your social group, yet you never knew who it was in that group that actually wanted them there.

Most people would take such a comment as a joke, a tease. But it was never like that from Piper. It was always for some menacing purpose, some underhanded remark designed to knock away at one's self-esteem.

"You go hit on her then," Dalton said, trying to make a

joke, trying to keep the conversation light – but he could already see Brooklyn reddening.

Out of everyone, Brooklyn seemed to hate Piper the most.

"Nah, not my type," he claimed. "I can do better."

"Let's see it then," Brooklyn demanded. His joking façade had fallen off like a cheap mask, replaced with a stone-cold grimace. Dalton could already feel Brooklyn's knee battering up and down beneath the table.

"What?"

"Let's see it, Piper. This great bird you can get, this sweet piece of something nice you keep locked away that none of us ever see."

"Yo, mate, I was fucking teasing."

"Nah you weren't, though, were you? Y'never are."

"I don't see no birds going in and out of your room at night."

"Yeah, but I don't go around claiming to be Billy Big-Bollocks, do I?"

"Go fuck a duck, man."

Brooklyn turned to Dalton, sharing a look of *can you believe this guy?*

"Brooklyn, don't, mate," Dalton urged him, but it faded to noise.

"Fuck a duck?" Brooklyn repeated. "What the fuck even is that? Who says that? What does that even mean, fuck a duck? You come out with some shit."

"So do you."

"Shut up, man."

"Make me."

"Quiet your noise, mate, or I will fucking make you."

"Let's see it then."

In a sudden movement, Brooklyn stood, batting his tray of food in Piper's direction.

Dalton could see the anger in Brooklyn's body – the tight fists, shaking arms, reddening of the face. If he breathed fire, Dalton wouldn't be surprised.

"Come on then, dickwad. Fucking try it!"

Dalton stood, put an arm out to Brooklyn, placing it gently on his shoulder.

"Come on, mate," Dalton said, quietly, calmly. "He's not worth it."

Brooklyn grabbed hold of Piper's collar, who allowed himself to be helplessly pulled across the table, destroying his lunch as he did.

Brooklyn held his fist back, Piper squinted, and Dalton put his hand on that fist and his other hand on Brooklyn's cheek.

"Come on, mate; let's go. Yeah? Let's go see if we can get you some water or something."

Without a word, Brooklyn took Dalton up on his allegiance, turning and walking out like an ape with puffed cheeks.

"Well done, Piper," Dalton muttered over his shoulder. "You really are a dick."

Dalton led Brooklyn away.

Brooklyn had a temper, that much was true. But, deep down, Dalton was still glad that, despite the situation not calling for such hostility, Brooklyn still had his back.

NOW

Every step Cia took toward the Sanctity was another step toward the storm that surged inside her. A heavy feeling of foreboding filled her, and she decided she did not want to go through with it.

"I don't know about this," she said to Dalton. They were trudging over another muddy field as Boy ran ahead to look over all the different tree types they were approaching.

"Don't know about what?" Dalton asked. Cia knew he knew what she meant, and wasn't quite sure why he was asking for clarification.

"Going back to the Sanctity, I just..."

She thought about how she could phrase it. How she could articulate her concerns.

*I'm worried because I'm responsible for the death of every righteous prick that lived in there while I had to struggle to survive outside it.*

*I'm worried because the last time I was here I watched my father face his demise as the rest of the people fled to certain death.*

*I'm worried because I think I may blurt this out to you, and that would change everything, and I don't want things to change because I...*

What?

*I what?*

She shook her head to herself.

"I just... I have a bad feeling about this."

She wasn't lying. She did have a bad feeling about this.

"Why don't you and Boy wait outside for me? I can go in alone, I won't be long."

It was appealing.

God, it was appealing.

But how could she let him go in alone?

How could she risk losing him now that she'd found him?

"I'm not leaving you," she said. "I'm just...worried."

"What is it you're so worried about?"

Her hand grew suddenly warm. She looked down to find that Dalton had slid his hand into hers, his fingers interlocking with her fingers and his grip tight, like he wanted to hold on, like he needed to hold on.

She hated it and loved it both at the same time.

But it did something to her.

This was nothing she'd ever done before – holding hands with a man, that is. And not only did it take her by surprise, it made her whole body shake with nerves. It was exciting yet terrifying. Perfect yet anxious. Immaculate yet filthy.

"I'll be fine," he said. "*We'll* be fine."

She looked ahead to Boy, in his own world, speaking aloud to no one in particular as he darted from tree to tree.

"That's a Black Alder, and that is Ash. Ash is the third most common tree in the United Kingdom. This is another Ash. Which one is this? Ah, yes, look at its leaves, toothed, and with an asymmetrical base that tapers to a sudden point at the tip."

"He's remarkable, isn't he?" Dalton said.

"What?" Cia knew who he was talking about, but she was still feeling flustered and wasn't quite as astute as she normally was.

How was it, just a simple touch of his hand did this?

She felt silly.

She'd fought monsters and men, she had killed and she had won more battles than luck could afford her...

Yet, just his hand sliding into hers, and all those actions melted into the obscurity of memory, and she was a whole new person – angelic and complete.

But it was wrong. It all felt wrong.

Because he was standing within a mile of the truth, and it was a truth that could kill both of them.

"Wow," Dalton said. "How can he do that?"

"Wh – what?"

"Boy. Just reciting all these facts. He's remarkable."

"Yes." Cia smiled. "He is."

"I mean, I struggle to remember most things. Sometimes I even forget how to tie my own laces. I mean, it comes back quickly, but there's sometimes a pause. Boy – the way he can remember all these things..."

"He is incredible." She turned a smile toward Dalton. "I wouldn't have him any other way."

He leant in. She panicked. As if picking up on her panic, he rested his lips on her forehead, ever-so briefly, but long enough. And he whispered:

*I wouldn't have any of this any other way.*

She lifted her head and, for the first time, their lips met. It lasted for seconds, but for Cia, it lasted a life time.

She didn't want it to end, but it had to.

He pulled away and smiled and she tried not to let on

how scared she was, how vulnerable he'd made her, and how much her body was shaking.

It was more than just a kiss; it was the feeling that she was part of a family again, that she was part of a team.

They kept walking, their fingers still interlocked. They passed a small cottage with walls stained with moss, a crumbling thatched roof, and a few smashed windows – but, despite its imperfections, Cia still couldn't help but admire its beauty, falling in love with its daintiness, its picket fences leading to field after field.

"That's a really nice cottage," she thought aloud.

"Really? It looks a little rundown."

"It's lovely." In a sudden change of thought, Cia turned to Dalton with sudden fright. "What about people?"

"What do you mean, what about people?"

"In the Sanctity – what about people? What if there are squatters, or people who have found it deserted and claimed the territory?"

"Then we deal with them."

"How do we deal with them?"

Dalton stopped, bringing Cia to a stop too. She checked on Boy, who had paused further ahead, inspecting a tree trunk.

"Put your arms up," Dalton instructed.

Cia lifted her arms.

"No, like this." Dalton demonstrated a boxing stance.

Cia copied.

"Right, now imagine I go over your head once, upper cut next, what do you do?"

"I – I don't know."

"You duck duck swing."

"You mean, like duck duck goose but violent?"

Cia regretted the joke as soon as she made it. Still, Dalton laughed, so it wasn't too bad.

"I guess. Let's try. Duck."

He threw an arm toward her head and she ducked it.

"Duck."

He went for an uppercut and she ducked, dodging to the side.

"Then swing."

She brought her arm up and playfully knocked Dalton beneath his chin.

"You got it," he said.

Strange, how she'd never thought of the need to fight before. She'd confronted evil people in this perilous world, but she'd never actually had to engage in hand-to-hand combat with them. So far, she'd been wily enough to find other ways to win.

But if this made her feel a little safer...

"And look, if we get separated while we're down there, or if we get separated any other time, then that cottage will be our rendezvous. That's where I will meet you."

She looked back at the cottage, sitting solitary with nothing around it. She wished that they would just set up home in there now and forget the Sanctity.

But she was starting to learn that she had little choice in where they were going.

"Rosy!" Boy shouted. "Come look at this tree!"

Cia smiled at Dalton.

"We need to keep moving," Dalton urged.

"I know, just give him five minutes."

Five minutes.

That was all.

Five minutes until forever.

# CHAPTER SEVEN

The rain beat down in bullets against the entrance to the Sanctity. It was as if the storm had been waiting for the Sanctity to enter Cia's vision; because, just as it did, the sky sent missiles of water into tiny detonations upon the surface.

Boy hated the rain.

He hadn't had a breakdown in quite a few days, but the immediate bombardment of fluid ammunition crashing against his skin was enough to send him charging toward a nearby tree. He used its thick branches as shelter, pressed against the trunk, eyes closed, ears covered, rocking back and forth.

Cia felt like joining him.

The door to the Sanctity poked out of the ground so nonchalantly, as if it wasn't a strange eyesore in the middle of the Lake District.

It was the same door that Cia had entered unconscious.

It was the same door that Cia had fled from days later.

It was the same door where a man, holding a gun, told her she wasn't allowed in with her father. Her father, who went in anyway. Her father, who never returned to object to the racist, elitist bastards who wouldn't let a helpless mixed-race child into their underground cult.

As familiar feelings surfaced, any worry or concern or hesitance as to whether or not she'd done the right thing in freeing those creatures and tearing this place apart flooded out with the rain.

Dalton approached the door. The bottom half was jammed shut and the top half was bent outwards, as if something had fought against it and twisted the metal out of shape.

Dalton twisted the door handle to find that it didn't open. He barged against the door a few times, rattled the door handle. Eventually it opened.

"Hang on," Cia said. "Let's stick together."

She walked over to where Boy was sitting, still shaking, still shutting his eyes.

She placed her hands on his wrists. Not with force or strength, but with a gentle touch, just to let him know she was there.

Using as little force as she could, she tried to take them from his ears, but he made his arms stiff.

She leant her forehead against his.

Didn't move his wrists. Didn't get cross with him. Didn't even talk.

Just held herself in that position, softly rubbing his wrists, pressing her forehead firmly, but with a softness he couldn't help but sink into. Just letting him know she was there.

Eventually, his moaning stopped.

She was able to take his hands away.

His eyes stayed closed, but it didn't matter. She cupped his face in her hands, held it, skin on skin, letting him know she was there.

That she was not going anywhere.

"It's okay," she whispered. "It's okay, Boy."

Keeping his eyes shut tight, he shook his head with a stubborn vigour.

"The devil has departed..." she spoke, keeping her voice melodic and unthreatening. "And you are not alone..."

He finally opened his damp eyes.

Lifted his gaze to hers.

He looked so young. So vulnerable.

"See that door over my shoulder? The one where Dalton's standing?" Cia said, feeling Dalton's stare burning into her back.

Boy nodded.

"That's where we're going. That is all the rain we have to run through. It will take us seconds, I promise."

Boy nodded.

"But I'm scared, see," she told him. "I'm scared that the rain will get me, and I need you to hold my hand as we run there. Will you do that for me? Will you hold my hand?"

Boy nodded. "Of course."

"Come on then."

Taking hold of his hand, they jumped to their feet and ran the few yards to door held open by Dalton, the few steps through the rain soaking them. He shut the door behind them.

Dalton handed Cia a flashlight that she passed on to Boy, then handed her another, then took one for himself. Their shafts of light switched on and they jumped.

This was the top floor. Blood still stained the walls, and a few limbs still decorated the floor. Even though dreaded remnants still obscured the walls, there were a few squatters. Survivors with big, grizzly beards, sleeping bags, wide-eyes. None of them threatening, all appearing scared.

"Easy," Dalton said, loud enough just for Cia to hear. "Slowly does it."

He was advising her like they these squatters were wild animals close to pouncing. Still, he was right – humans could be just as dangerous as the creatures. She had to be cautious.

It didn't take long until they had crossed the room and reached the door that would lead them to floor one – the top floor.

Cia decided she could handle the top floor.

With a surge of bravery, she may even be able to descend lower into the Sanctity and brace floor two, maybe even three.

Floors four and five were even a possibility.

But no lower.

*Please, Dalton, no lower...*

Just as Dalton opened the door, one of the squatters stood and shouted.

"Don't!"

Dalton turned his gun and pointed it.

"Don't hurt me, I mean you no harm," said the man. "It's just – you don't want to go down there."

Dalton didn't care what this man had to say. But Cia did.

"Why?" she asked.

"There are things down there. Those creatures. At night, we hear noises..."

Cia glanced at Dalton, who looked undeterred.

"I lost... I lost my son to them..."

"Dalton," Cia whispered, urging him to consider turning back.

"We'll take it under advisement," Dalton said, keeping his gun held high and walking in.

"Maybe we shouldn't," Cia said.

"They aren't like us," Dalton insisted, and stepped through the door. "We are prepared."

Cia grabbed hold of Boy's hand as tight as she could, and

he gripped back. Reluctantly, they followed Dalton into the facility.

## CHAPTER EIGHT

It was an ocean of remnants. A lake of violence. A complete sea of viciousness they had to cross, hoping the choppy waters didn't sink them.

Dalton lifted one foot after the other over bits and pieces of people he once knew, using the walls of the corridor to balance himself, placing his fingers on the brief patches of metal vacant of stains. He looked where he was going, except for when he passed the few bodies that remained slightly recognisable; those were the ones from which he had to avert his gaze.

He'd seen a lot of bad things in his time. He'd become immune to a lot of it. He'd shot at people in the army and he'd seen his comrades fall, but he'd never had to endure a sight such as this.

This used to be his home.

His *home*.

*This used to be my goddamn home.*

Now it was just a graveyard of incoherent faces, abhorrent, discarded leftovers, and memories of a place now destroyed.

How had this happened?

How had those creatures escaped from such a secure unit to do this?

Then he saw him.

The face he never wanted to see yet wished that he would.

Laying across the corridor, eyes wide open.

"No..." he choked.

But what did he expect?

He knew how Brooklyn had died. He'd known this was where it had happened. What – did he expect his eyes to somehow lie to him?

Brooklyn had been a unique man; but, looking around, Dalton could see there was nothing unique about his death.

He felt Cia's eyes on him. Cia, who was talking so adamantly to Boy, doing all she could to divert Boy's attention from the despair that their eyes could not escape.

In that moment, Dalton did not care.

This was the world they lived in now.

He fell to his knees beside Brooklyn's face. The face that still looked up at him, beseeching him with his vacant eyes, his face void of any more happiness or misery.

"No..." Dalton wept.

He held in his tears, though.

Brooklyn wouldn't want any tears. He'd always said, *man tears are not for men.*

Poor advice, really. A man should cry, not bottle it up. But that wasn't what Brooklyn had believed.

There was a lot about what Brooklyn had believed that Dalton didn't necessarily agree with, but that he would never verbally object to. He was just happy for Brooklyn's company. Despite all his misgivings, the loyalty Brooklyn had shown him was rare.

As if to repay this loyalty, Dalton gently placed his palm upon Brooklyn's eyes, closing his eyelids so it just looked like he'd taken a nap.

That's all it was.

A nap.

Sleep time.

That's what he could tell himself.

But, looking around the rest of the floor, it was clear to see that Brooklyn wasn't the only one sleeping so soundly.

Brooklyn's chest was open. Part missing. Like he'd been fed on.

But Dalton remembered: *Brooklyn had been dead long before any creature had managed to use him as dinner.*

We should all be so lucky to be granted a quick death.

"Goodbye, Brooklyn," Dalton whispered, and stood.

# CHAPTER NINE

Cia watched Dalton with a hesitant intrigue.

She had been so busy talking to Boy about anything she could think of to keep his mind off the sight of the corridor – trees, dinosaurs, even food they were hoping to find – but she'd still kept her gaze on Dalton, curious about the one particular body Dalton was hunched over.

Despite how much she distracted him, Boy's eyes still kept lingering. He'd have look of trepidation as his eyes would hover over the discarded pieces of human, and Cia would have to ask a new question with renewed enthusiasm, just to keep him occupied. Just to keep him thinking about other things.

But Boy was shaking. The fact that he hadn't had a meltdown was evidence of how accustomed he'd become to the world they now lived in – but, as much as he'd been exposed to, he hadn't been confronted with such violence in such epic proportions in such a little corridor, the walls of which were even starting to close in on her.

"It's okay, Boy," she eventually said, breaking the pretence of trying to divert his attention, and just admitting to what they could see. "It's okay. I see it too. It's horrible. But it's okay."

Dalton was still on his knees beside the body, brushing his hand gently over the dead man's face so as to close his eyelids.

Dalton took a moment.

Whispered, "Goodbye, Brooklyn."

Then stood.

"Who was he?" Cia asked.

Dalton didn't reply, at first. He stood with his head down. His face was directed at the body, but his eyes were directed elsewhere.

"A friend," Dalton finally answered.

"What was his name?" Cia asked.

Dalton sighed.

This seemed to be really troubling him.

What was it about this guy that had Dalton so morose?

They were surrounded by a mass of death, yet this one person stuck out to Dalton amongst all the other people he may have once known.

"Brooklyn," Dalton said. "His name was Brooklyn."

"Like the place in America?"

"Sure." Dalton let out a sad chuckle. "Not that I've ever been. Nor him. But yeah, like the place."

Cia kept one hand in Boy's as she stepped toward Dalton, pulling him closer.

She sunk her spare hand into his, not holding it at first, but just letting their hands meet. Once his hands had met hers, she clamped her fingers around his and squeezed, a gesture she knew would mean a lot to her should it have been the other way around.

Should it have been him that had killed all of her friends.

*Stop it.*

He forced a smile that was less than genuine, but she took it. It was more than she had expected.

He let go of her hand and trudged on. Creating a route that she and Boy could follow, stepping over the leftovers.

Cia smiled at Boy, kept hold of his hand, and guided him.

"Is Dalton okay?" Boy asked.

Cia hesitated.

No, he wasn't. But how could she explain that?

"He's just sad," she told him.

"Why?"

"Because one of the people on the floor used to be his friend."

"Oh."

A moment of silence went by.

"Am I Dalton's friend?" Boy asked.

"Of course."

"Would he be sad if I died?"

Cia stopped and turned to Boy.

Dalton must have heard, too, as he stopped and looked back at them.

"Why would you ask such a thing?" Cia beseeched him, cupping his face in her hands the way she often did.

"I don't know..."

"Of course I would be," Dalton spoke up. "I would be devastated."

Boy looked to Dalton, a wounded expression upon his feebly young face.

"Really?"

"I don't know how I'd go on without you, buddy."

"But no one's going to die," Cia urged him. "Not you. Not Dalton. And not me. You hear?"

Boy nodded.

She saw in his face that the corridor was starting to get too much. The sight that he'd tried to reject was now seeping through. The best thing for them to do would be to just get out of the corridor and back to the stairs.

"None of us are going to die," she repeated. "Now come on, we better–"

A clatter interrupted her sentence.

All three of them abruptly turned their attention to the far shadows of the corridor.

Dalton lifted his gun.

Cia withdrew her knife.

Another clatter.

Something was there.

# CHAPTER TEN

Eat.

Hungry.

Smell.

Fresh smell.

Not decay.

Fresh smell of people.

Hungry.

Run.

*These are the thoughts of a Waster.*

A Waster, one of the absentminded people who sacrificed their consciousness to be allowed to live, but to live as a slave to the creatures.

A Waster, whose sole drive was to eat.

And these cannibalistic bastards could smell like a wolf.

Damn, could they smell.

And they had smelled nothing in these corridors but death and decay and rotting for so long.

Now something smelled fresh.

It was approaching. It was above them.

It was enticing.

Hungry.

Smell.

Eat.

They looked to each other. Their blackened eyes beneath their greasy hair that fell upon their filthy shoulders. Their grubby, barely-covered bodies, with skin wrapped tightly around their bones, like string around a joint of beef.

Grunt.

One grunted to the other.

They grunted back.

Grunts swept down the rest of them.

They had been scavenging for so long and now there was fresh meat.

They were all starving, and there was enough to go around.

Run.

Run after the smell.

Unison.

All together.

Despite their absent minds their instinct allowed them to coordinate, to synchronise. Their muffled shouting displayed their celebration, conveyed their excitement.

Fresh.

It's fresh.

Still alive, maybe.

Breathing.

But not for long.

No, not for long.

They ran.

Bashing against the wall of the corridor.

Beating the door open with their heads and feeling concussed as the surge of bodies behind them carried them forward.

Battering their feet up the steps as the smell grew stronger.

Closer.

Getting closer.

So close.

Can almost taste it.

Salivating.

Drooling.

Appetite wettened. Desperate. Starving.

Up more steps. Smell stronger.

They reached the floor where the smell was the strongest and they sniffed it in, sniffed it deep, and barged through the double doors.

Oh God the smell was so strong.

So strong.

So hungry.

So hard.

Maybe it was a girl.

Maybe it was a strong man with lots of muscle to eat.

Maybe there was more of them.

The smell grew so strong. So, so strong.

One of them closed their eyes and took it in, the way one would with a beautiful roast dinner that smelled of cold Sunday afternoons.

They wouldn't even cook the meat.

God, no.

Too hungry for that.

Can't wait.

Can't wait any longer.

Just dive on them and feast.

Feast upon them.

Turning the corner, a few shafts of light shone in their direction.

The smell punched them in the gut and they enjoyed the pain.

Ooh, yes.

Dinner was served.

On a platter.

They surged forward, reaching out for their dinner, reaching out for the three fools who dared descend the steps into the Sanctity.

# CHAPTER ELEVEN

CIA KNEW what they were straight away.

Their sound was unmistakable.

The uneven, limping steps of their chaotic run, the unmistakable body odour, and the fading grunts.

*Wasters.*

Their torch beams shone in the direction of the clatters; clatters that promptly smashed the far doors against the wall and turned to feet beating against metal.

"Run!" Dalton screamed.

Cia grabbed Boy's hand and dragged him forward, but he remained like dead weight.

"Hey!" she said, grabbing his face that was stuck, in awe, in the direction of the approaching shadows. "No one's going to die, remember?"

He nodded.

"But if we want to stay true to that, we need to run. Come on!"

She pulled harder and eventually he stopped resisting.

She was momentarily grateful for how much easier it was to make him move than it once was. There was a time when he'd stay rooted to the spot and they'd have had no choice but to hide.

Unfortunately, there were few places to hide in a corridor.

Cia refused to let her legs slow down to Boy's pace, instead coercing him to hurry up. It seemed to work as he was keeping pace, even though he was struggling.

Dalton was, however, starting to run too far ahead. He stopped and turned back, waving his arm to urge the others to hurry.

Dalton's eyeline became momentarily directed over Cia's shoulder and, from the look on his face, Cia could tell that he'd seen them.

She didn't need to look back.

She knew what they looked like.

She could smell their revulsion; their clammy, greasy skin. She could hear their disgusting, heavy breaths pushing closer.

Dalton aimed his gun and fired. A few slaps against metal occurred, but the falling bodies did little to deter the rest of the footsteps.

"Head for floor three!" Dalton shouted.

Cia was confused. Why floor three?

She kept running, the far doors to the stairs coming into sight.

She glanced over her shoulder.

She didn't know why, but she did.

And she regretted it.

Even in the darkness she could see them. Faded, cracked skin. Beady, black eyes. Cheeks covered in drool.

And this was the first floor.

This had been a huge mistake. Why couldn't they just leave?

"What's on floor three?" Cia asked, shouting over the approaching snarls.

"CCTV!" Dalton answered. "We can lock the door and I'll watch them, wait for them to leave!"

It was logical.

Even if it wasn't the truth.

"Fine!" she concurred.

They reached a set of double doors that led to the stairs. Once they had burst through, Dalton found a discarded arm and shoved it through the door handles.

The Wasters' faces plastered against the small panel of glass and the door buckled.

They ran down the stairs. They knew the Wasters wouldn't be held for long, but it could give them enough time to get to the CCTV room without any of them seeing where they'd gone.

But they'd smell them. Cia knew that. They'd smell them.

But were Wasters absentminded enough to not search the rooms?

Were they stupid enough for that?

*I hope so...*

They reached the double doors to floor three. Pushed. They wouldn't open.

They heard the door above collapse.

Dalton kicked against the doors and they narrowly opened, revealing the pile of bodies on the other side wedging the door shut. Dalton kept kicking and eventually created a gap big enough for them to push through.

He waved Cia and Boy through.

"This way!" he instructed, leading them into the corridor and around the corner.

The doors behind them bashed open.

Dalton found the CCTV room, knocked the door open and allowed Cia and Boy inside, closing the door and turning the lock.

Then they stood there.

Waiting.

Listening.

The sounds were there. Grunts, grumbles.

The heavy steps passed through, pursuing false shadows further down the corridor, and eventually fading.

They were safe.

For now.

From the Wasters, at least.

Cia turned to Boy, who was hyperventilating.

He used the wall to steady himself, evidently dizzy, finding his way into the far corner, where he curled up into a ball and began making that noise – a distressed moan on each outward breath.

Cia turned her back to the mass of CCTV monitors, a few of them cracked, and crouched before Boy.

"Boy, you need to stop making noise, they'll find us."

But he didn't.

He just continued.

And, with Cia not paying any attention to anything else in the room but Boy, Dalton turned the CCTV system on and began searching for the day that the Sanctity fell.

# THEN

# CHAPTER TWELVE

Sometimes it felt like he lived in the armoury, such was the time Dalton there; sorting weapons, preparing weapons, and choosing weapons.

As it was, he and Brooklyn were preparing to do a perimeter sweep. There was always a risk they'd come into contact with something nasty, but Dalton had done enough of these sweeps to not feel nervous about it anymore.

Besides, if anything happened, he knew Brooklyn would have his back.

"What you thinking?" Brooklyn asked, sifting through weapons.

"I'm taking the assault rifle."

"The Diemaco 17?"

"Yeah, what you going with?"

"The Glock 17."

"Seriously? Don't you want something a bit more powerful than a pistol?"

Brooklyn grinned. Dalton had just walked straight into that one.

"Mate, it ain't about the size of the pistol – it's the way you shoot the load."

Dalton shook his head to himself. Sometimes the constant stream of sexual innuendos grew tiring. Yet he knew that, with Brooklyn, they would always be part of the 'lads club.' Dalton had never really been much of a 'lad' – not that he'd ever admit it to Brooklyn.

The door to the armoury opened and another private walked in – Private Stacey Harvey. Long, blond hair, dazzling smile, and "breasts you could balance a beer on" as Brooklyn always proclaimed.

Instantly, he knew how Brooklyn was going to act with Stacey, and felt embarrassed before he'd even said a word.

"Ah, Stace will know," Brooklyn claimed, his grin growing even wider.

Dalton rolled his eyes.

*Here we go...*

"Know what?" Stacey asked, picking up and assembling a L128A1 Combat Shotgun.

"This is my pistol," Brooklyn said, holding his Glock 17 in the air. "Pretty small, ain't it?"

"I guess." Stacey frowned, not quite getting the point.

"I was just saying to my man, Dalton, over here – that the size of the pistol ain't important. It's the way you fire it. You get me?"

Stacey shrugged. Pulled a *leave me alone* face that Brooklyn seemed oblivious to.

"You ever, er, let someone shoot their Glock 17 all over you?" Brooklyn asked, accompanied by a wink.

"Jesus, man," Dalton said, finally repulsed enough to say something. "Leave the poor girl alone."

"Girl?" Stacey repeated. "Try woman."

"Yeah, sexist," Brooklyn mocked.

"And I don't need you sticking up for me," Stacey continued.

"Fine, fine!" Dalton waved his hands in surrender, wondering how he'd ended up the bad guy.

"You know," Brooklyn continued, and Dalton let out a long, exasperated sigh. He really, truly hated it when Brooklyn was like this. "Once we've finished circling the perimeter, I was wondering if I could circle your perimeter?"

Stacey finished putting together her shotgun, placed it over her back, and began searching the boxes for the correct ammunition.

"The only perimeter you'll be circling," Stacey said, pressing a sarcastic smile against her face, "Is your own."

"Oh, you wound me!" Brooklyn joked.

Dalton thought that would be the end of it.

But it wasn't.

"Come on, babe, let's get serious – you and me, let's make this happen, yeah?"

Brooklyn stepped into Stacey's personal space. She backed away, but the wall stopped her from escaping, and he was close enough for her to smell the eggs from his breakfast against her face.

"Get away from me," she demanded.

"Aw, come on, don't tell me you never thought about it."

Stacey looked to Dalton expectantly. As if he was meant to do something. Which confused him, as she'd made it perfectly clear what she thought about his intervention.

She finally found the ammunition she needed. She pulled it out, having to press herself unwillingly against Brooklyn to do so.

"Yeah, that's it," Brookyln said in a deep, gruff voice he put on, his lecherous grin growing more and more disgusting.

She pushed him away.

"You're a pig," she said, then left, slamming the door.

Brooklyn turned and smirked at Dalton.

Dalton wondered what he expected. Applause? An encore?

"That wasn't cool," Dalton said, more quietly than he intended.

"Aw, come on." Brooklyn smacked him playfully on the shoulder. "The world's gone to shit, may as well have some fun!"

Brooklyn led Dalton out and they began their ascension to the top floor.

At least, outside the Sanctity, there would be no one for Brooklyn to start a fight with or sexually harass.

NOW

# CHAPTER THIRTEEN

Should the Sanctity have still been operational, CCTV footage would have been archived after a month, then deleted after three to make way for more storage.

As it was, with the facility having been abandoned, the final recording had come to an end when the storage became full, two days after the Sanctity fell. It didn't take much effort for Dalton to readjust the time. He used one screen, out of the many screens available, to play back the beginning of the day that the Sanctity fell. He fast-forwarded to the appropriate hour.

Heavy feet stormed past the door. The door knocked under the barges against the wall, the metal fort shaking under the tremble of the footsteps, the screams and grunts growing louder as they passed.

But no one tried to get into this room.

For now, at least.

He turned the screen away from Cia, and edged behind it.

He didn't know why he was doing this.

Somehow, he felt like this needed to be a secret.

But what was he being secretive about?

He glanced at Cia. She was kneeling next to Boy, who was still moaning and panting and turning red and teary. He looked like he wasn't going to break out of his trance-like meltdown any time soon.

Once Dalton had readjusted the time, he readjusted the camera. He searched for the camera in the bottom level, and eventually the screen displayed various creatures bound with chains and tubes pumping depressants into them.

He'd never thought about it before, but he found the image slightly unnerving. To see so many creatures being treated so cruelly. The creatures would kill and eat them given the chance, yes, but humans ate pigs and cows – doesn't mean they were deserving of being bound and gagged because of it.

Come to think of it, it had been exceedingly dangerous having so many of these creatures within the facility in the first place.

There were so many of them. The room was huge, but still overcrowded. Thorals, Masketes, Wasters – even a Lisker, a creature so rare Dalton had never seen one in the flesh.

Then again, they had been kept there for four years without incident. There couldn't have been a malfunction on any equipment, it had all stood so strong for so long, there couldn't have been, surely...

"How are we looking?" Cia asked between attempts to calm Boy.

Dalton quickly recalled telling Cia that he was watching the Wasters outside the room, waiting for when they left.

"They are still there," Dalton said. He wasn't lying about that, they probably were – but that wasn't what he was watching.

He didn't feel guilty for his deception.

Why didn't he feel guilty?

That was the first time he'd ever been dishonest with her.

"I don't think we should try to get any food," she decided. "I think we should just leave when we can."

Dalton watched her. So young. So pretty. And so powerful.

"Fine," he said, quietly.

She turned back to Boy and continued talking to him, as gently as her voice would allow.

Dalton watched as the monitor continued to show these creatures held against their will, but held securely.

Just as they had been for a long time.

Doctor Daniel Rose walked in.

Cia was with him.

With her father.

Both in protective gear.

Had she watched him die?

Had Cia had to watch her father die?

He bowed his head. He'd never thought of that.

*Poor Cia.*

Suddenly, he did feel guilty for being deceptive. She'd never spoken of her father or what had happened down there. They had just been reunited, and then...

Daniel and Cia walked between the creatures. He was saying something, but he couldn't see their faces from the aerial view the camera showed.

Someone came over to Daniel and spoke to him. He signalled something to Cia, then went off with this person for a moment.

Then Cia walked toward the Lisker. Slowly, but with an aimless curiosity.

She stood beside it, looking the Lisker up and down.

It was subdued, drugs pushing it into submission, but she was still too close to it.

What the hell was she doing so close?

He looked over to her again, still badgering Boy.

Why had she been so close?

He looked back to the screen.

Cia reached out a hand and placed it on the Lisker. Its rough skin was harsh and sharp, and it must have pricked her finger, as she quickly withdrew her hand.

Then she did something he couldn't fathom.

She took out a knife.

She held it in the air.

Someone shouted something and everyone looked at her.

Her father looked at her. Shouted.

She shoved the knife into one of the tubes pumping chemicals into the Lisker.

# CHAPTER FOURTEEN

"Hey, hey," Cia kept saying. "Listen to me."

It was no good.

Boy was deep into one of his episodes and snatching him out of it was going to be difficult.

But she needed to snatch him out of it – if he wasn't ready to go when the time came, they would be screwed. Dalton was adamantly engrossed in the CCTV, watching, waiting to give them the go ahead to run – and Boy needed to be ready for when that moment came.

"Shush, come on," she said.

Why was she finding this so difficult?

Boy had been so much better recently. Yes, he'd had his moments, but she could normally snap him out of them relatively easily.

This one seemed to be drawn out, like there was something worse, something deeper, something that was unsettling him.

They had been chased by monsters before.

Numerous times.

Then she realised – it must be the Sanctity. The last time

he was here he'd been bound to a chair for days, possibly weeks, tortured and prodded at and tested and analysed, so-called doctors vehement that he had been in contact with something that could cause some kind of infection.

The only vile infection Cia had ever seen spread was humanity. People were the disease.

"Hey, look at me," she urged him.

His eyes closed and his head dropped, but she grabbed his cheeks and lifted his head to hers.

He kept his eyes closed, refusing to open them, to lift his head. It was as if, when he couldn't process something, he shut down and went into denial that it was happening. He couldn't take this place, and therefore, he would rather pretend he wasn't in it.

"How are we looking?" Cia asked, turning briefly to Dalton.

Dalton paused, then said, "They are still here."

"I don't think we should try to get any food. I think we should leave when we can."

Cia's eyes lingered on Dalton's.

It was a strange kind of gaze.

She didn't see Dalton in his eyes – which was a bizarre thought to have, as it was evidently Dalton. His skin, his face, his body looked the same. Yet something was gradually morphing.

Then he broke the stare and seemed to come around.

"Fine," he said, and turned back to the screen.

What was up with him?

Boy began to moan louder. She covered his mouth.

"Please, Boy, we are hiding, you can't make that noise or they'll find us."

His eyes widened, as if to say, *you mean they will find us?*

That was the wrong thing say.

She grabbed the back of his head and pulled him in close, resting her forehead on his, keeping her hand pressed firmly against his mouth, not bothered that her fingers were now becoming wet.

"Listen to me," she whispered. "I know it's this place you don't like. I don't like it either. But the only way we can get you out is if you calm down."

He seemed to calm down a fraction, his noise seemed to lessen, though his stomach was still inflating and deflating at a worrying speed.

More noises screamed past the door, and another one of them bashed into it.

He went to scream, but she pressed her hand firmer.

"No!" she shouted in a whisper. "No noise, Boy, we can't make any noise."

He nodded.

"You understand?"

He nodded.

"Can I take my hand away now?"

He nodded.

He looked back at her with such weak eyes.

She knew he wanted to say something like, *I'm scared,* or, *I can't take this.*

Problem was, he wasn't able to fully understand those emotions, let alone verbalise them. So she had to verbalise it for him.

"You're scared," she told him. "You think you can't take this. Right?"

He nodded.

"Well you can. You are strong, Boy. So strong. You can beat this place. We both can."

This place.

*This bloody place.*

It was cursed.

She hated it.

Nothing good had ever happened here.

She turned to Dalton.

He was staring at her. Why was he staring at her?

And why was he staring at her like that?

"Are you okay?" she asked.

But he just kept staring.

# CHAPTER FIFTEEN

"Please, Boy, you can't make that noise or they'll find us."

Dalton blanked out Cia's voice as he kept watching her figure on the screen.

Her father was running toward her now, still shouting after her.

Cia was standing still, so still, next to this Lisker whose eyes were beginning to open, whose body was beginning to twitch.

Everyone looked up, as if there was a noise – Dalton realised that was the point when the emergency voice started telling everyone to evacuate.

In the instant when that voice started, everyone except Daniel and Cia ran out. People shoved off their protective gear, barged others out of the way, fleeing for survival.

Daniel and Cia were saying something to each other. Shouting something. Cia was leaning forward, so aggressively – he'd never seen her like that, but she was going for her father, screaming at him almost. He was arguing back, but she was the dominant one in the argument.

Was all of this because of some feud with her and her father?

The Lisker's body shook. Its head began to rise.

Its tail rose and bashed into another room, smashing the room apart, destroying the glass and the beakers and the test tubes and all the hard work accumulated over years.

The Lisker battered its tail once more, smashing the wall above a Thoral, and consequently unleashing it.

"Listen to me," he heard Cia whisper to Boy. "I know it's this place you don't like. I don't like it either. But the only way we can get you out is if you calm down."

Get out of this?

A place she doesn't like?

She damn well destroyed it!

The screen showed Cia finally moving, her father following, and they ran with Cia in front, toward the shutters that were slowly descending.

Cia was running far faster, getting closer and closer to escape.

He was stumbling, struggling to keep up.

The creatures were beginning to scream. The Wasters opening their mouths at Daniel streaming past, Masketes battering against their chains.

More clumsiness from the Thoral freed more creatures.

She reached the shutters first.

A Thoral slammed its paws down beside Daniel, and the tremble of the ground caused him to fall.

He reached his hand out for his daughter.

From his place on the floor he reached his hand out, stretched it as much as he could.

She stood, motionless, from a point of safety, just watching him.

Watching him helplessly reach.

And she did nothing.

Absolutely nothing to save her father.

"No noise, Boy, we can't make any noise."

The shutters fell almost to the ground.

"You understand?"

The Lisker was liberated.

A large group of Masketes fell upon Daniel and started picking at his body.

Cia just stood there. Still not moving. Just watching. So cold, so stationary.

"Can I take my hand away now?"

The Masketes shredded Daniel and within seconds he was in five or six parts.

Cia watched the whole thing. A blank-faced voyeur.

And then the shutters reached the bottom, and all he could see on the screen were the creatures escaping through the adjacent rooms they had battered down, and pieces of Doctor Daniel Rose left strewn across the floor.

"You're scared. You think you can't take this. Right?"

He turned and looked at her. His head a slow rotation, his neck the only thing moving. He watched her as she so lovingly took care of Boy.

"Well you can. You are strong, Boy. So strong. You can beat this place. We both can."

They can beat this place?

She already had.

The conniving, backstabbing, treacherous...

She turned and looked at him. Met his gaze.

He didn't falter in his glare.

His expression stayed the same.

And, for the first time since he met her, he was looking into the eyes of a stranger.

"Are you okay?" she asked.

He didn't answer.

He had no coherent thoughts. No articulated response. No perfectly formed act of vengeance.

Just feelings he couldn't yet fathom, and knowledge he couldn't yet comprehend.

How could...

Why did...

What should...

Nothing formed. Nothing lasted. Nothing could register.

Boy had finally calmed down.

She was still looking at him.

He had nothing to say.

"Are they gone?"

He robotically clicked off the monitor. He hadn't looked, but the noise outside the room had gone. It was safe.

Without saying a word he charged to the door, opened it, and, seeing that the coast was clear, left.

She followed.

## CHAPTER SIXTEEN

Cia kept her eyes loosely attached to the back of Dalton's head as he led them out.

Though 'led' was the wrong word – it felt far more like she and Boy were following him, rather than him leading.

Something about the way he had looked at her had shaken her. Frightened her. It was a look she'd never seen from him before – usually, his gazes at her were warm, full of adoration, occasionally cheeky.

This one seemed cold. Disconnected. Like he was looking at her from far away, where he was actually looking at her from across a small room.

She went to pause at the corner of the corridor, ready to peer round and check what was there before running into it.

Dalton didn't.

He charged around the corner, his gun pointed, recklessly pursuing forward.

What was going on?

"Dalton!" she called out.

He didn't turn around.

She took hold of Boy's hand tighter, pulling him forward,

increasing pace, trying to keep up with Dalton. He seemed to be marching on ahead like he didn't care if they were up with him.

But he did care. He was so caring. He never did anything without checking on her and Boy's safety first. Just like she did with him – they took care of each other. They were a team.

"Dalton!" she tried again, but he simply turned another corner.

Ahead of them, a single Waster crouched over an unrecognisable corpse, pulling what they could out of its open chest.

It looked up at them, sniffing, its eyes wide.

Cia halted, ready to hide, ready to consider the course of action.

Dalton took aim and unloaded a long succession of bullets at the Waster's head. Even after the Waster was flat out on the surface, Dalton carried on firing at the spasming body until his ammunition was empty.

He took more ammunition from his belt and put it in.

This was a stupid move. Cia knew it.

They were in a metal box. The stream of bullets were still echoing long after they had finished.

Who knew what may have heard it.

Cia looked over her shoulder, expecting something to come running, to hear the noise of Wasters.

Very, very far away, on a floor far below, thudding sounded.

"Dalton!" she cried out.

"What?" he snapped, turning around to look at her.

"What the hell are you doing?"

"I'm killing a Waster. Is that an issue?"

"That's what we have knives for! God knows what beasts you may have attracted!"

Dalton took a few sinister steps before her and she had to resist cowering.

"Yeah," he snarled. "Wouldn't want to be trapped in here with something evil, would we?"

She looked into his eyes, still devoid of empathy, and could not figure out what was behind them.

"What is wrong with you?"

"What's wrong with me?" He shrugged. Stuck out his bottom lip. Looked around as if mockingly searching for an answer. "Nothing. I'm fine. What's wrong with you?"

She felt Boy grip her hand.

"You're scaring him," Cia said, just as scared as Boy was.

"Why? The Waster's dead."

Distant thudding became slightly less distant.

"They heard it."

"Heard what?"

"The gunshots."

"What, like these?"

Dalton trudged back to the dead Waster and unloaded another round of bullets into the corpse.

"Stop it!" Cia shouted, her voice breaking against the might of her scream.

He smiled. Not a nice smile – but a smile that went with his eyes.

"Let's just get out of here," Cia said. Whatever this was, it would pass.

Or would it?

Suddenly, she realised how little she actually knew Dalton. What small amount of time she'd known him.

No.

That couldn't be true.

They had spent every minute of every day together. She knew him inside out.

And this wasn't him.

"You want to get out of here?" he repeated.

"Yes!"

He marched forward and Cia followed, and they stepped into the staircase.

"Dalton slow down!"

"I am slowing down."

"What is wrong with you? Why are you–"

She stopped talking.

A gigantic roar from below them interrupted her.

She looked below them, peering down the stairs, and saw a Thoral looking back.

# CHAPTER SEVENTEEN

He considered, for a moment, not running, and not fighting.

Just letting the Thoral make its way up.

Letting it devour them.

Letting it eat them up and keep them in this damned pit forever.

Doing to her what she did to everyone else.

Doing it to himself.

After all, he could have easily perished with the rest. He could have easily died amongst the masses.

Did she care about that when she unleashed those monsters?

*I bet it didn't even cross her mind.*

"Dalton, we need to go."

Taking the cue, he turned and walked up the stairs. He stopped marching or running; instead, he began trudging, meandering slowly, in the way of Cia and Boy.

The Thoral's roars grew louder. He could see its shadow rising upwards, ascending the floors, pounding up the staircase.

He'd forgotten how horrible they looked up close. How big they were. How bloody their drool was. How blackened their eyes were. The sharpness of their claws.

They were evil in the form of a monster.

He looked at Cia.

*Just like you.*

"Dalton, why aren't you running?"

Why wasn't he running?

Huh.

Dalton hadn't deliberately made the decision to stop running,but he had made the decision, nonetheless. Perhaps somewhere in the hostility of his subconscious.

Cia looked down. Dalton didn't.

He didn't have to.

He could see by the look on her face, the tears forming in the corner of her eyes, the way she was clutching onto Boy.

Onto Boy, not him.

She went back for Boy.

After she put this place into chaos, she went back for Boy. Dalton just so happened to be there to help.

If he hadn't, they wouldn't have escaped together. She wouldn't have spared a second thought for him, and he'd have died with the rest.

And now she was holding onto Boy, not him.

Boy was her reason for living, not him.

Boy would always be her priority.

*Why do I even care anymore?*

The stairs shook, scraping apart. The Thoral's paw swiped out, and the steps a few floors down detached and fell into the nothingness.

"Dalton, please."

He looked at her.

Her face. Such a young face. Innocent, but not. Vulnerable, yet conniving.

But she looked scared. Truly scared.

And it pained his heart, and he hated himself for it.

So he ran, and they ran with him.

The Thoral barged its way up to the steps. Bashed its way upwards. They made it to the top floor, but as they sprinted across the room, the Thoral burst out behind them.

Luckily for them, the dwellers and the squatters were slow to react. With those susceptible few between them and the Thoral, they managed to gain ground as the Thoral devoured the helpless survivors.

How simple, really. All they'd had to do was outrun the weaker of their species; to reach the door before the Thoral had finished feasting.

Dalton felt bad.

He was basically putting these poor, starving people to death, so they could escape.

They had led that thing up there and now it was their fault these people were dying, and Dalton hated it.

He wondered if Cia felt the same.

She didn't even look back at them. Didn't even flinch.

He did. He peered back to see the poor morsels ripped apart and shredded.

Her eyes were solely on the exit.

He reached it first, ahead of them. He ran through it.

Then he looked back. The Thoral still making its way through the innocents.

Her and Boy yards away.

He went to close the door.

Considered it.

What if he did?

What if he shut the door on them and left them in here?

Forced Cia to die... Forced her to watch Boy suffer...

Would he feel bad, like she didn't?

Before the thought had come to a conclusion she ran through and shut it behind them, trapping the others in.

She looked briefly into his eyes.

Then she continued running, her hand still clamped around Boy's.

He followed.

# CHAPTER EIGHTEEN

Cia clutched onto Boy for dear life, never letting go of him, never letting them get separated.

They had been separated last time they were at the Sanctity.

Not again.

Never again.

Dalton paused as they fled the door. Perhaps he was considering whether they should shut the squatters in. But he didn't need to, Cia shut the door for them. She didn't do this trap the squatters – she did this to shut the Thoral in.

From the look of it the squatters hadn't survived anyway. Their lack of speed to react was unfortunate but, just as she was beginning to feel bad, she reminded herself: *This is the world we live in now.*

Those who aren't ruthless and quick end up dead and eaten.

She didn't condemn those people to death. They could have run out too. They could have followed them, and she would have done her best to lead them to safety.

As it was, she, Boy and Dalton were the only ones to make it to the door.

Her brief look into Dalton's eyes told her that he didn't feel the same way.

Was that it? Was that what was going on?

No, it couldn't have been. He'd been acting strangely before that.

They carried on running, and the whole route grew dangerously familiar. Without conferring, they found themselves running the same route they when they'd fled the Sanctity six months previous. Maybe it was habit, maybe it was automatic, or maybe it was just what they knew – they did not stop running until they were miles enough away and were sure that the Thoral hadn't followed.

They stopped at a tree, where Cia placed her hand and bent over, panting.

Boy sat under the tree, tucked his arms around his legs, and stared. Didn't moan, whine, or collapse – just stared into nothingness.

Dalton stopped. He didn't move. He went from running to completely immobile in a second and stayed there, as if there was no in between.

And he was so still.

So, so still.

He didn't even pant, or have to calm his breathing down.

He just stood, his fists balled up, his face morphing betwixt confusion and anger. Something was bothering him and he wasn't going to say what it was but it was tearing him up.

Then Cia remembered – his friend. Brooklyn. He'd seen his dead body, just before they went into the CCTV room.

Was that it?

Was that what was bothering him?

It was the only thing Cia could think of, and decided to try and be more understanding. It can't have been easy for him to see anyone he knew torn up on the floor, let alone someone he may have cared about.

Once her panting had resided, she walked over to him and placed her hands on his arms. She felt small, covered in his shadow. Nothing but his eyes reacted, turning to look at her as if she was a stranger, but that was okay – if that was how he wanted to deal with grief, she had to let him.

She had to be there for him, just as he was for her. And Boy.

"What was his name?" she asked. "Brooklyn?"

His eyebrows moved a fraction, as if to narrow slightly, a tiny frown.

"I'm sorry you had to see him like that," Cia said honestly. "What can I do to help?"

He still didn't react.

He was so damn still.

And she wondered whether it was Brooklyn, or whether she was wrong.

Whether it was something else he'd seen...

She reached her hands up and placed them on his cheeks. Just like she did with Boy. Just like she would do with both of them.

She smiled at him. Even if he didn't smile back, she smiled at him, showing him that she was there.

She glanced at Boy to check he was okay. He was fine. And she turned back.

"We don't have to keep walking if you want," Cia said. "We can rest here. I can get some twigs and logs and build a shelter. It will be fine."

He closed his eyes and sighed. A negative response, but a response nonetheless.

"Hey," she said, turning his face and forcing him to look at her. "I'm not going anywhere. I'm still here."

He swallowed.

Breathed deeply in and out.

And nothing else.

Knowing what she would want in this situation, she did the best thing she could.

She leaned in and placed her lips ever so gently upon his.

# CHAPTER NINETEEN

HE KEPT HIS LIPS TIGHT. Didn't withdraw, but didn't go forth. Just let her plant those smooth, perfect, bloody spectacular lips against his.

He didn't kiss back.

She didn't need him to.

He just watched her, eyes open hers closed, hovering as she rested them there, pressing lightly, enough to be a kiss but not enough to force it.

Allowing her to be a leech, sucking on his soul.

He wanted to cry and scream and cackle and punch all at the same time.

But he kept it inside, turned it into a batch of resentment he could build upon and build upon and build upon and build...

She was still there.

He wasn't doing anything, but did that not seem to matter to her?

She just took.

Took what she wanted.

He loved the kiss, and hated himself for it.

It infected him.

A loving evil.

He hated her and he desired her.

The kiss both gave him chills and intensified his wrath.

Up and down his body he felt beautifully dirty.

Why was she doing this?

Did she think this could fix anything?

She thought it was his best friend's death that was bringing out this hostility.

But he'd already known Brooklyn was dead.

Dead, just like everyone else in the Sanctity.

Only, he hadn't realised that it was *her* who had killed them.

Her hands pressed against his cheeks. As if she had to hold him there. As if she had to keep him in place.

As if that was the only way.

Or were those hands hiding the world from him? They were beside his eyes so he could see nothing but her.

And then the kiss ended.

She looked back at him with a smile, triumphant in its success, as if that just cured everything. As if her lips were the enemy of grief.

As if they could nullify any pain he felt over a fallen comrade.

"I'll get some wood."

She left to build the shelter.

"I'm going to leave you with Dalton for a bit, okay?" she said to Boy.

She kissed him on the head before she left.

See? There was nothing special *about me.*

He was alone with her most treasured asset. Her prize possession. Her only real love.

What could he do to that *only real love* now to cause her pain?

*She is a cretin.*

Malevolent.

Sinful.

And yet, she was still all he had.

# CHAPTER TWENTY

The kiss was cold.

He didn't react, but that was fine.

She didn't need him to.

To be honest, she wasn't even sure if his eyes were closed.

She kept her hands upon his cheeks, gripping harder, letting him know she was there. She hovered, held her kiss.

The kiss still sent her into a tizz. Sent her reeling into a world of mania.

She hoped that these kisses could last forever.

But he was still cold. The kiss was not reciprocated.

But that was okay.

We all deal with grief in different ways.

Maybe she just needed to leave him alone. Give him a bit of time. Let him be in denial, be angry, start to bargain, get depressed.

Then, eventually, once acceptance had landed, they would be what they were again.

"I'll get some wood," she told him, figuring they were probably going to have to shelter there for the night.

She should probably take watch for most of it. Let him sleep.

This would be the first time in the open. Just like they used to. Under the stars, close enough to touch but nervous enough not to.

She walked up to Boy, who was doing so well, and gave him a kiss on the forehead, letting him know that she was there for him too.

"I'm going to leave you with Dalton for a bit, okay?"

He nodded.

Dalton would still take care of him. He'd never let anything happen to Boy.

Dalton would die for Boy, just like her, and that was how she knew Boy would be safe.

She left to find some wood.

THEN

Just as he'd gotten dressed that morning, brushed his teeth, and eaten his breakfast, Dalton walked the perimeter on automatic. Both he and Brooklyn had walked it enough times that it didn't require much deliberate thought. They walked leisurely with their guns at their sides, listening astutely whilst rambling on.

Brooklyn often spent the walks rattling on about the pointlessness of them, and this time was no different.

"I mean, there's no way anyone'll find it, is there?" he kept going, louder than Dalton would have liked considering what could be lurking nearby. "No one'll find the door and, even if they do, no one'll get in. No survivors that is – as for creatures, they won't even know what it is. Just doing this is pointless."

"I know," Dalton agreed, even though he really didn't. "But if it helps everyone to sleep at night, then whatever."

"Pah! The point of that place is that we can all sleep at night without any idea what's going on out here. Yet we have to be subjected to it. That's all they want us for."

"Good."

"Eh?"

"I just mean, good, they want us for something. Imagine where we'd be if they'd never found a use for us."

They passed the same leaves, avoided the same nettles, stepped over the same logs. The same distant lake ran, the same birds cooed in the sky, and the same menacing silence hung over them with a readiness to be broken at any time.

"Hey," Dalton said, catching Brooklyn's attention.

There was something...

Beyond the trees...

It didn't look to be moving.

It looked like a person.

Brooklyn saw it too and, in unison, they both raised their guns. They approached whatever it was and, as it came closer, it grew clear that it was a woman. Leant against a tree, her back to them, not moving whatsoever.

"M'am?" Dalton said. "M'am, are you okay?"

Brooklyn scoffed.

"M'am?" Dalton asked, Brooklyn laughing at his politeness.

Dalton shrugged.

"Oi!" Brooklyn shouted. "Speak up now or we'll fucking shoot you."

Dalton flinched.

"Did you hear me? We're talking to you, bitch, answer!"

"Brooklyn, mate," Dalton said, keeping his gun firmly raised, but allowing himself a glance of disgust in his friend's direction. Brooklyn returned the glance with a snigger.

They rotated around her body, both of them approaching from a different side until they were facing her.

She was slumped, palms up, skin pale, crusted blood masking her face.

They both dropped their guns, then covered their noses as the stench of decay hit them.

"Jesus," Brooklyn exclaimed.

"Looks like she's been dead a while."

"Yeah, no shit."

Brooklyn walked up to her and prodded her with his foot.

"What are you doing?" Dalton asked. "Knock it off."

"Why? She's dead, what does it matter?" He kicked her again. "Jesus, she's like solid brick."

"It's called rigor mortis."

Brooklyn swung the gun over his back and placed his feet one either side of her, his crotch in her dead face.

"She looks like she was a pretty little thing, don't she?"

"Fuck, Brooklyn, show some respect."

"Oh, I respect. I respect the female form in its sexiness, dead or alive."

Dalton felt like gagging. He almost did. He turned his head away and winced, repulsed at the sight of Brooklyn gyrating his crotch before a set of eyes stuck open with dried blood.

"Let's just go," Dalton said, but his request was ignored.

"Got a hell of a pair of tits, too." Brooklyn reached his hand down her top and grabbed hold of her breast. "Gross, that's stiff too."

"Well it is going to be stiff."

Brooklyn turned around and grinned. "Not the only thing that's stiff."

"Come on, mate, this is sick."

"Just a moment, my friend."

Dalton placed his weight on one leg and looked to the sky with a huff. He hated it when Brooklyn was like this. Who was he showing off to? It was just them. Brooklyn had no audience, had no women he was trying to impress or blokes he was trying to out-macho.

Then he heard a trickling sound, and hoped he was imagining it.

But he wasn't.

And he turned around to the sight of Brooklyn's dick in Brooklyn's hand and the woman's face fresh with urine.

"What the fuck, Brooklyn?" Dalton exclaimed.

Brooklyn turned to Dalton with an even bigger grin.

"Relax, she's probably into it."

"She's dead! What is wrong with you? How would you like it if someone pissed on your dead body?"

"Wouldn't give a shit, mate, I'd be dead."

He finished up, shook his penis to ensure the final drips landed upon her lips, then zipped himself up and stood back to admire his work.

Dalton couldn't move. Nor could he shut his open jaw, and nor could he understand what he had just witnessed.

Brooklyn swung his gun back into his hands and began walking again.

"You coming?" he asked nonchalantly.

"Are you – how – why–"

Dalton had no idea what to say.

"What? Thought you wanted to keep going?"

"What about – are we not going to acknowledge what you just did?"

"What?"

"That was someone's mum. Someone's sister. Someone's daughter. And you just – what the fuck!"

"Mate, she *was* someone's daughter. Now she's just a hot piece of dead ass." He shot a bullet into her chest. "See? Dead."

Dalton shook his head.

He loved Brooklyn like a brother. Brooklyn always had his back.

But sometimes, there were these moments…

Moments where he wondered whether this world they found themselves in was created for someone like Brooklyn.

"You coming or what?" Brooklyn asked, a fair few paces ahead.

Dalton began to walk and paused by the woman's body – considered shutting her eyes, showing her some respect, but didn't want his hands in Brooklyn's urine, so just walked on.

And they kept walking on until they arrived home and Brooklyn seemed to have forgotten the whole thing.

NOW

# CHAPTER TWENTY-TWO

DALTON'S EYELIDS were like weights. They kept dropping down over his dry eyes.

Yet he didn't feel tired.

Just drained.

He'd been up most of the night. He knew Cia was keeping watch, but who was keeping watch on her? She checked for the monsters, and he checked for the monster.

He was walking about ten, twenty yards behind them. Unnoticed. Unthought of.

Or so it seemed.

Cia and Boy had run ahead. Playing like two children. Just to look, you wouldn't have known Cia was caring for Boy. You would have assumed it was both of them that were stupid and inept.

He rubbed his eyes.

His thoughts were poisonous.

He was grouchy and he knew it. He hated everything. He felt like telling the sun to fuck off and go back to hiding behind the clouds. Should a Maskete swoop upon him now he would raise a middle finger and tell it to go ahead, try it, see what would happen.

Of course, the Maskete would win, but Dalton didn't care as he already felt defeated.

He watched her. Prancing around, giggling, cackling like a witch and he hated it because he had started to love her hard, hard, a strong and rampant affection he hadn't been able to control and hadn't wanted to and now she'd ruined it she'd ruined it she'd ruined it *she'd goddamn ruined it.*

No, it had always been ruined.

It had always been wrecked.

He'd only just realised it now.

They stopped beside a bed of flowers. Perfectly grown, beautiful sunflowers, with grand yellow petals and an amber tint to its centre, perfect for a bee to come and pollenate.

She stuck her nail into the neck of the flower, picked it off and handed it to Boy.

They both laughed.

Her and Boy.

And he wished he would stop calling him Boy.

His name was James.

Boy was a pathetic name to give him; a stupid, idiotic, childish decision. Call him by his name, his name, his actual goddamn fucking name.

"James," he grunted.

Cia looked over her shoulder at him.

"What did you say?" she asked. Fluttering her eyes and smiling her smile and nursing the dead head of a flower between her dainty fingers.

He could bite of that finger with the strength it would take to bite off a carrot.

"Nothing."

Her smile grew into wary smile. Pleasurable to concerned.

She looked like a doctor with a patient she was delivering bad news to.

He used to have a doctor. Someone who cared for him and checked him over and made sure his health was in order.

Cia had killed him.

"Are you okay?" Cia asked, her voice so concerned, so genuine, so wicked.

"I'm fine."

"You just, you don't seem fine. I know it's hard to see Brooklyn like that—"

"Don't say his name."

She paused a moment. He could see it in her eyes, she was deciding whether to bite.

But she never bit.

Not with him. She was always so nice. So kind. So caring.

So perfect so wonderful so evil fucking liar liar liar liar lair *fucking liar*.

"Your friend," she said, changing her words.

"Rosy, I found another good one!"

Distracted by Boy's voice, she left a lingering stare on Dalton and walked over to Boy. Abandoning Dalton for Boy – *not his actual name* – once again.

She crouched over the flower bed beside Boy.

"Oh wow, that is a big one!" she said, looking at the biggest, prettiest sunflower of the whole bunch.

She clipped off its head and gave it to Boy, who seemed so happy.

"You just going to murder that, too?" Dalton asked.

"Excuse me?" she asked.

He was muttering. If he wanted to be heard, he had to speak louder.

But did he want to be heard?

"Flicking the head off the petal."

"Did you want one?" she said, smiling cheekily, sexily, playfully, insinuating he was jealous because he was being missed out.

"No," Dalton answered. "No, you don't need to kill anything else for me."

He turned and walked away.

He could feel her watching him.

He could feel himself loving her.

He could feel himself hating himself for it.

# CHAPTER TWENTY-THREE

Cia kept her distance from Dalton for the rest of the morning. Yet, occasionally, as they were walking through the shade of the towering trees, she would glance at him and wonder what was going on beneath the surface...

Something about him seemed...off.

Like something had changed inside of him. Like something had begun to eat away at him and corrode his soul. Like the person he was, was now...

No, he was still Dalton.

She had to support him. Had to be there.

Beside her, Boy knocked his leg into a log and the sunflower heads he had gathered in his hands spilt over the ground, discarded by the wind.

She could feel Boy's tears coming before they arrived, and she already had her hands wrapped around him.

"It's okay, Boy," she reassured him. "We'll find more. It's okay."

She looked up, expecting Dalton to say something. This would normally be when he'd interject with something calming or reassuring, something like, "It'll be all right, kid," or, "Here, I'll get you some more."

She half-expected him to already have gathered another handful by the time he reached her.

But, as it was, he stood still. His face pale and empty. Standing over them, just watching.

She held his gaze.

At least she tried.

His eyes didn't meet hers.

They were different.

Dead, almost.

And, for the first time since she'd met him, she felt fear, and she realised – she was terrified of the man she loved.

# CHAPTER TWENTY-FOUR

Cia didn't sleep next to Dalton, like she always had.

Normally they would be side-by-side. She'd be lying there, thinking about touching him, too scared to move, knowing he was probably thinking the same thing.

Sometimes, their hands would meet, and they would fall asleep with their fingers intertwined.

Now, there was a considerable distance between them. She was closer to Boy than she was to Dalton.

Boy, who was obliviously dreaming. Not snoring, but breathing deeply – enough for Cia to know his mind was far, far away.

She envied him. To be clueless as to what was happening was a luxury she craved.

Then again, did she really know what was happening?

She reached her pupils to the far side of her eyes to peer at Dalton. She didn't turn her head, she didn't want him to see her move, she just strained her eyes as far as they would go.

She couldn't quite see him, lying across the shelter they'd created, but she could see enough to know that his eyes were wide open. He was lying stiff, like a board, wooden, glaring above him.

What was he thinking?

What was going on in his mind?

How had this Brooklyn guy's death affected him so much?

Maybe it wasn't that.

Maybe Brooklyn's death wasn't the cause of all this.

She tried to think. Pushed her mind back into her memories. It was just a day ago, yet it seemed far back in history. At what point had he changed?

It was when they left the CCTV room.

He had stared at her.

He'd looked at the monitor, then looked at her with a look she didn't recognise.

Had there been something on the monitor?

Something he'd seen the Wasters do as she tried calming Boy down?

What could the Wasters have–

Then a thought occurred.

How did she know he was looking at the Wasters on the monitor? He could have been looking at anything.

He could even have been looking at...

No, of course not. It had been months. CCTV would have been erased by now, surely.

Then again, how would it be, if there was no one there to erase it?

Her actions could well have been one of the last things to have been recorded. Etched into the vast space of the hard drives like a bad tattoo, scarred and itching to be scratched.

But for Dalton to have searched out that footage...

It was unlikely.

But possible.

After all, wouldn't she want to know what had happened? What had caused it?

Wouldn't she have wanted to see exactly who was responsible?

She looked over at Dalton. Not just with her eyes; this time, she turned her head. She wanted him to know she was looking at him. She wanted him to turn his head and let his eyes meet hers.

She wanted to look into those eyes. She knew, once she looked into them, she'd be able to tell. She'd be sure – whether he knew the truth or not.

The truth.

Secrets.

Withheld honesty was a deadly burden. It was a snake more poisonous than a Lisker, scratching at her insides, carving its words beneath her skin.

And he could probably see those scars now, could probably see those words.

He could see who she really was.

What she had done.

Then again, why would he still be here?

If he knew, why would he still be following her? Why wouldn't he have left?

Or worse – why wouldn't he have killed her? Exacted revenge?

She knew that if anyone hurt Boy, she would destroy them.

After all, she already had, hadn't she?

The Sanctity fell. She had a lot of resentment, but it was witnessing what they did to Boy that had given her the final push. That had made her...

She was being silly.

She knew that.

She shook her head, shook herself out of it.

He didn't know. Of course, he didn't.

He was grieving.

She just needed to be there for him. Show that she wasn't going anywhere. Show that, no matter how much of a prick he was being, she would not desert him.

This was a horrible world they lived in now.

And they required each other's support.

Even so, she did not wish to sleep. She did not wish to leave herself vulnerable. She wasn't sure enough to give up her awareness.

She vowed to stay awake, but eventually tiredness took her, and she fell into a reluctant slumber.

# THEN

## CHAPTER TWENTY-FIVE

It took a lot for Dalton to be able to push his way into the segregation unit.

It was supposed to be unvisited. Isolated. So that those being punished could be left alone.

But there was no way that Dalton was letting Brooklyn rot away in a tiny room with a wooden slab for a bed and a pot for his shit – not after what Brooklyn had done for him.

Brooklyn's actions had been stupid, yes, but still – it was Brooklyn's interpretation of loyalty, however misguided his actions were.

As he waited for the verdict as to whether he'd be allowed in, he ran through the afternoon's events once more, helplessly picking apart what he could have done differently; at what point he could have asked Brooklyn to stop, begged him to come around.

But no, Brooklyn had his own misguided stubbornness that no one could change.

"At ease!" the general had said, marching down the corridor.

All the soldiers on floor three had stepped out of their

rooms and stood to attention. Now, at the general's prompt, they separated their legs and placed their hands behind their back. They stood in a row, obediently dormant as General Hark patrolled the space before them, inspecting their beds.

It all felt a little bit...childish. Like they had to have their beds analysed for creases. There were monsters outside the Sanctity, killing people, as they had done the vast amount of the world's population, and here they were having to stand in silence as some pompous, self-righteous arsehole checked whether they had made their beds in sufficient time.

"Okay," Hark muttered as he passed one private's bed.

"Yes, fine," as he passed another.

He paused beside Dalton.

"What's this?" Hark demanded.

"What's what, sir?" Dalton responded with his face stiff and his voice confidently compliant.

"This shit sty you call a bed?"

Dalton glanced over his shoulder. His bedsheets were somehow untucked and his pillow skewwhiff. He must have missed it.

"Did I tell you to look at it?" Hark barked.

Dalton turned and faced ahead again.

"No, sir."

"So tell me, what the hell is this?"

"I don't know, sir."

"Do you not know how to make a bed?"

"I do, sir."

"Then why is it such a fucking mess?"

Dalton hesitated. Allowed himself a sigh he knew would only incense Hark. Hark didn't want an actual answer, he just wanted to show Dalton up, and Dalton knew he just had to ride it out.

"It's just a bed, sir."

"What!" Hark shouted, moving his face so close to Dalton's he could smell the tuna from last night's dinner.

"I mean, with all respects, I don't consider a crooked pillow to be that important," he said, then made sure to add, "sir."

Hark retracted a baton and, without warning or cause, swung it at Dalton's leg. Dalton moaned in agony as he fell to his knee.

"Let's have it better next morning," Hark instructed, then moved along to the private next to Dalton: Brooklyn.

Brooklyn's bed hadn't been touched at all. It was a mess. Completely unmade.

Which was strange, as Dalton could have sworn he'd seen Brooklyn making his bed that morning.

"Your bed is a state!" Hark observed. "I didn't see it like that when I came in!"

"I know, I just messed it up while you were badgering Dalton – *sir*."

"You what!"

Brooklyn waited a beat and looked around.

"Was that a *you what* to demonstrate your disbelief, or are you actually deaf – *sir*?"

"How dare you!"

"With all respect – or not, you know, don't really care – what you just did to Dalton was really unneeded, and I ain't being drawn into no battle about my bed when there are people outside being maimed alive – *sir*."

Hark went to swing his baton, but Brooklyn caught Hark's wrist and held it there.

Hark's eyes widened into fury. Shock adorned his face at the impudence of this miscreant.

"Get out of this room," Hark had demanded.

Dalton shook himself out of the memory. Stopped

thinking about it. He'd already replayed the scene many times and nothing had changed, the events still occurred as they had the last time he recalled it.

"Fine," said the private. "You have five minutes. If Hark catches you, I didn't let you in."

"Thanks," Dalton said, grateful that it was his friend that was on duty.

He made his way through the corridor until he reached a big slab of metal with a tiny square displaying a few bars.

"Brooklyn," he said, banging the door. "Mate, it's me."

There was shuffling, then Brooklyn's face appeared at the square.

Dalton recoiled at the sight. Brooklyn's face was covered in the darkest of bruises, blood had dried beneath his nose and one of his eyes was squinting.

"Shit, what did they do to you?" Dalton asked.

This was wrong. That someone could do this to another person...

Then again, whose rules were they living by now?

He immediately desired a way to exact his own revenge, to stick up for Brooklyn like Brooklyn had for him.

But there was no way. Nothing he could do. Not an action he could take that he wouldn't shy away from.

Brooklyn was a unique kind of warrior, always fighting the impossible battles he chose for himself. He was very different to Dalton in that way – Dalton, who was only in the army to survive.

"It's fine, you should see the other guy," Brooklyn joked.

"I'm being serious, mate, this is – this is wrong. It's barbaric."

"Barbaric? Woah, you been reading a dictionary or what?"

Dalton went to snigger, then decided not to demean the graveness of the situation.

"We have to do something about this," Dalton asserted. "Tell someone, or report it, or something, I don't know."

"Oh yeah? Let's see how that works out."

"But – why? Why did you do this? Why put yourself in this position? You're going to be in here for days, maybe even weeks, looking like shit."

"Are you seriously asking me why I did this?"

"Yes, I am!"

Brooklyn's face turned to a beaten happiness. His smile was weary, but strong too.

"Why did I do it?" He shook his head to convey the ridiculousness of the question. "Isn't it obvious?"

Dalton shrugged. No, it wasn't.

"I did you for you, Dalton," Brooklyn said. "Because you're my brother. I'll always have your back."

NOW

# CHAPTER TWENTY-SIX

Dalton could feel himself slipping away.

He didn't know what he was doing.

He'd awoken absently, with little sleep, and now he was continuing to trudge behind Cia, glaring at the back of her head.

Anger had taken over.

Somewhere inside, he was still there, but his voice was small and his will was weak.

This was who he was now.

A quivering wreck.

A man morphed to a boy who did not know what to do.

All that love he had felt for her, all that affection, that caring, that deep unaltering passion – where was it?

It was still there, cuddled up in a small circle with a circumference made of antipathy.

She put her arm around Boy.

She didn't look back. Didn't put her arm around him.

Put her arm around her *favourite*.

She'd killed for Boy. She'd done everything for Boy that Dalton had sworn he would do for her.

He bowed his head. Rubbed his head. Ran his hands through his greasy hair. He was sweaty. Dirty. Filthy. That didn't help.

He considered shouting ahead that they should find a river to wash, but he didn't want to speak. Didn't want to engage, converse, or interact.

Why was he even still there?

If he meandered off now, she wouldn't notice. She wouldn't look back and see that he wasn't there. She wouldn't grieve his missing. She'd move on.

She wouldn't move on from Boy.

Her prized possession.

Who did she think she was?

Dalton realised he couldn't go on like this forever. Just trudging behind them every day, resenting her more, growing in his hostility.

He either had to leave, or...

Or...

Or what?

What else did he have to do?

What could he do to Cia that would possibly show her what she had done to him?

*Boy.*

Perhaps if she felt that loss, she would feel something close to what he was feeling.

Would she still follow him around if that's what he did? If he made them even?

Would she still meander behind like he was doing now?

Or would she turn back into that sadistic killer and...

Was she a sadistic killer, though?

Had she even thought it through?

If her father hadn't been there, if Boy hadn't been tortured, if...

If.

If.

If.

*Shut up.*

*Ifs* never solved anything.

He felt for his knife, tucked into the back of his belt.

He felt for his gun, swung over his shoulder, gently batting against his waist.

She was a sweet girl. A young woman. A fighter.

A carer.

A lover.

A bitch. A psycho. A *liar*.

Why was he doing this?

Constantly attempting to mentally depict it, to compromise with himself, to convince himself of what he didn't really think, tell himself she was not like that, but was she was she was she he didn't know didn't know what to think what to think what to think she.

Killed.

Everyone.

Not with her hands, but with her actions.

And now she carried on like she didn't even care.

She had to pay.

*She has to.*

She ruffled Boy's hair. Squeezed him tighter. They laughed about something.

Not looking back at him.

Just the two of them.

Two of a kind.

Two of a pack.

A couple against the world.

*I can't go on like this forever...*

There was only one way to find his reprieve.

This was the world they lived in now.

Cia had already shown that.

This wasn't *The End.*

*The End* had already been and gone.

This was the ever after.

And now he knew what he must do.

# CHAPTER TWENTY-SEVEN

Cia was surprised to find she had survived the previous night.

At first, anyway – until she wondered what exactly it was she was expecting Dalton to do.

She knew he'd never hurt her.

At least, she knew that the Dalton of *before* would never hurt her.

She didn't know what the Dalton of *now* was capable of.

They'd come across what must have been a barn, next to what used to be a farmhouse but was now a burned-out building of collapsed wood. The barn was good enough for the night. Good enough until...

Until what?

Where were they even going?

She waited until Boy was asleep to raise the subject with Dalton. Whilst Boy nestled into a pile of hay, looking both cute and peculiar, she approached Dalton, who sat with his back to them, assembling and reassembling his gun, again and again, moving mechanically.

"Dalton," Cia said, making sure she didn't make him jump as she approached him.

He didn't answer.

"We need to talk."

She stood over him, and he didn't look up.

"Where are we going?" she asked.

Still no answer.

"At the moment we are just walking aimlessly. What's our next place? We've been to the Sanctity, now–"

His head abruptly turned around, his eyes peering up at her, glaring, as if the Sanctity was his trigger, like she had woken the beast inside.

A few days ago this would have startled her.

"What happened, Dalton?" she asked, hoping that if he had seen something on CCTV, now would be the time he spoke up.

He didn't.

His rigid neck relaxed, his head turned back, and he continued taking apart and reassembling his gun.

*Fine.*

She waved her hand in the air and left him to it. She found a good spot to sleep and lay there, staring at the ceiling, the broken wooden boards allowing in a few droplets of leftover rain.

The sound of the gun being constantly reassembled became a repetitive soundtrack to the monotony. She almost found a beat in it, a background noise to her anxiety.

In the end it sent her to sleep.

She was going to have to sleep at some point. If she didn't trust Dalton she needed to make a decision: leave, or stick with him – either way, she was going to have to sleep.

She sunk into a dreamless rest, thinking of nothing, having the kind of sleep most of us would crave.

She drifted and drifted, left this world in favour of nothing, sinking deeper.

Then the sleep abruptly ended.

Her eyes opened wide very suddenly.

And, looking above her, she understood why.

"What are you doing?" she asked.

Dalton's feet were either side of her chest. His body encased her in shadow, his menacing glare intensified by the darkness.

In his hand he clutched his knife, the blade pointed and ready.

"Dalton?" she said meekly.

He didn't move, didn't speak. Just stood there.

But his face... it was no longer empty. Now it was vile. Threatening. Intimidating. Multiple images of contorting agony.

"Dalton, what are you doing?" she tried again.

His blade dropped lower. He aimed it at her as if it were a barrel, and he were about to fire it.

Her whole body shook. Adrenaline ended any thought of rest. She tried to stay cool but no part of her could react, no part of her had any idea what to do.

"Please, Dalton," she said.

He went to one knee. Knelt over her, moving his blade an inch from her throat, back and forth, back and forth.

"Why are you doing this?"

Then the realisation hit her:

*He knows.*

It was the only certainty she could gain from this. No more deliberating, no more wondering, no more does he doesn't he...

*He knows... Oh, God...*

She slowly manoeuvred her own hand to her belt,

searching for her own knife. He hadn't removed it, which was foolish, which told her very clearly that he wasn't in sound mind: *he has no idea what he is doing.*

"Dalton," she said, slowly lifting her blade from its pouch.

He saw it and retracted his. He stood, looked over her again, his glare lingering.

"Get some sleep," he told her, and walked away, slowly returning to his sleeping place.

She looked over to Boy, a few yards away, asleep.

He was safe. Dalton hadn't done anything to him.

*Thank God...*

She made the decision. She had no choice. They had to leave. Get away from him.

For Boy's sake, if not for hers. They couldn't risk being around him anymore.

Right now, he was acting on anger and impulse alone – pretty soon, his plans would form some coherence and God knows what he'd do then.

He lay down, his eyes closed, his body still.

She'd wait until she heard him snoring. She'd wait until he was asleep, and she'd take Boy, and they would run, run far away, as far as they could.

She kept her eyes open and waited, not once letting go of her knife.

# CHAPTER TWENTY-EIGHT

She waited.

And waited.

And waited and waited and waited.

The worst part of the waiting were the thoughts. The constant stream of poisonous ideas running through her head, no sign of tiring, no sign of matching the weariness of her mind.

She watched Dalton, watched him close his eyes, waiting, thinking about the thoughts that must have been going through his mind over the past few days.

Had he seen everything on CCTV? Had he seen all her actions, what she had done, to her father and to the Sanctity?

How had he stayed with her after knowing this?

*God, he must feel so betrayed.* So hurt. Watching her, knowing what she'd done, seeing her happy afterwards.

She hadn't been happy. She hadn't been proud of it. She had done what her emotions condemned her to at the time. Everything had accumulated, her thoughts had overwhelmed her, and she'd just...

*Killed all of his friends.*

She bowed her head and stifled a tear. She didn't deserve to cry.

He deserved to be angry. Hell, he deserved vengeance.

But it wasn't Boy's fault.

*God, watching it on CCTV... It must have destroyed him...*

They had been falling in love. He'd kissed her, held her hand, saved her life, protected her and Boy.

And now...

He began to snore. A deep croak.

It was time.

She stood. She didn't go to take any of the food or water, they could find more, they just needed to get out of there, quickly, before Dalton stirred. She had no idea how deeply Dalton was sleeping and if they so much as snapped a twig at the wrong moment it could cost them their lives.

She crept over to the hay where Boy lay asleep.

She shook him. He groaned.

She looked over to Dalton, who hadn't heard it.

She covered Boy's mouth and shook him again. His eyes opened, widened, and she quickly put a finger over her lips to tell him to be quiet.

"Shush, Boy, listen," she whispered, as quietly as she could. "We need to get out of here."

He stared back at her.

"I'm going to take my hand away, but you can't make a sound, okay?"

He nodded. She took her hand away.

"No speaking, sound, or anything at all. Okay?"

She took his hand and stood him up.

"What about Dalton?" he asked in full voice, and she quickly covered his mouth again.

"Don't speak!" she demanded, then looked over at Dalton and back to Boy. "We have to leave him."

"Wh–"

She covered his mouth more firmly.

"No. Talking. Do you understand?"

He nodded. She took her hand away, slowly, gently.

"He's not coming with us," she told him.

His mouth began to open, as if ready to voice an objection, so she added an explanation; the only one she could think of that he would understand.

"Dalton has changed. He's not who he was. He's nasty now."

Boy frowned, as if to say, *but I really like Dalton.*

"I really like him too."

*I love him.*

"But we have to leave him. Or he might hurt us. Okay?"

Boy nodded. Very reluctantly, but he nodded.

She took his hand and guided him forward.

She checked back on Dalton.

He wasn't there.

He was stood up.

Before the entrance.

With a knife.

And his gun over his shoulder.

"Dalton?" she said, gripping Boy tightly.

He didn't respond.

Boy began to moan, fretting, staring at the knife in the hand of one of the few people he trusted.

Dalton moved Boy behind her and stood in front of her.

"Where are you going?" Dalton asked.

It had been a while since she'd properly heard his voice, and she'd missed it, but this wasn't his voice – it was deeper, like he had a cold, like he hadn't spoken in days and this was the first use.

She wanted to tell him she loved him. That he should stay. That she was sorry. That she wanted to explain.

But say she could explain – what then?

What could she possibly say?

No. There was only one solution to this.

"We're leaving," Cia said, then repeated it with more conviction: "We are leaving."

"No," Dalton replied. "You're not."

# CHAPTER TWENTY-NINE

"Dalton," Cia said, carefully, slowly, "What are you doing?"

"What am I doing?" he repeated.

She shifted her body ever so slightly to the side, until she was guarding Boy. She kept him behind her, her arms behind her, holding onto him, gripping onto him.

Dalton's crumbling façade terrified her.

He was shaking. He could barely keep that knife in his hand still. She dreaded to think where the bullets would go if he decided to use his gun. The whites of his eyes were scarred with red, bloody veins, his face was as pale as if he were dead, and his breathing was erratic, ill-timed, in and out in bizarre intervals.

"I've been thinking a lot for the past few days," he said. The shaking of his body had even found its way to his voice. It was mixture of extreme pitches, a quivering wreck.

This was not the Dalton she knew, or that she had loved.

This was someone else.

This was *something* else.

"Oh yeah," Cia said, just keeping him talking, keeping her eyes on the knife. "What have you been thinking?"

"About you. Who you are. What you are capable of."

The exit was behind Dalton. She had to get to it. Had to get to it before Dalton found a way to use his strength and take the action Cia once thought he would never take.

"What am I capable of, Dalton?"

"Stop talking to me like that," he said, an extra snarl to his voice.

"Like what?"

She edged further forward, closer to Dalton, closer to the exit.

"Like you're a fucking therapist! Stop talking to me all calm and, and, and fucking lucid, you're not, you're not that person!"

"What kind of person am I then?"

"A – a – a *killer...*"

Keeping her hands fixed around Boy's wrists, she came within steps of Dalton, keeping her eyes on his knife.

Then she stopped.

At some point they were going to have to make a move. Run or barge him or something and just hope for the best.

She felt Boy's hands on her waist. He was gripping back.

He was scared.

Then Dalton said those words – those words she was terrified of hearing ever since they began this wonderful life together.

"I know."

So matter-of-fact, so emotionless. The words were like a swipe of his knife, and yet there was so little passion behind them.

"Know what?" she asked.

"Shut the fuck up, Cia, you know exactly what."

She nodded. Confirmation. Tears accumulated.

"How long have you known?"

"CCTV. The Sanctity."

Of course.

*Dammit.*

He'd known all of these past few days. She was right – he had seen it. He had seen what she had done.

He had watched her as she did it.

Watching what she did to her father. To the Sanctity.

"They deserved it, Dalton," she said.

"What?" he cried, the clearest sign of aggression meeting his body. His whole torso tilted, lurched forward, his shaking arm gripping the knife tighter.

"Do you know what they did to me?" she said.

"What *they* did to *you*?"

"Me and my dad, the week it all happened – they let him in, but not me. Do you know why? Because I was mixed-race. They let my dad in, but not me, because of my skin. Do you understand that?"

Dalton just shook. She could see the conflict contorting his mouth, his nose, his eyes.

"Then they tortured Boy," she continued. "They attached him to a chair, didn't let him move from it, then did all kinds of things to him. It was inhumane. They took my dad from me, turned him into a person who chose that place before his daughter, then tortured Boy. Don't you see?"

He twitched. His whole head, then his body. He was shaking like he was freezing cold, yet perspiration soaked his face.

"Then they tied up the creatures, drugged them, in as inhumane way as they could."

"Those creatures are monsters!"

"No, *they* are the monsters!" she said. She was shouting now. "How were they any different?"

"So that means everyone deserved to die?"

"It was a crime of passion, Dalton. A moment of weakness, anger clouding my mind. I couldn't think of anything else. You don't know what it was like."

"A crime of passion?" he repeated. "Then I will use the same justification for what I'm going to do to you."

Dalton stepped closer to her.

"What are you going to do to me?" Cia asked.

"You?" Dalton shook his head. "You come second. First, I'm going to show you what it's like to see someone you loved be killed. I'm going to do to Boy what you did to me, and I am going to make you watch."

Cia withdrew her knife and held it by her side.

"Come any closer and I'll cut you," she said. Any assertion, calmness or attempt to think clearly had departed the moment Dalton had mentioned harming Boy.

Dalton just laughed. Guffawed, even. Mocking the suggestion that Cia could stand a chance against him.

She swung her knife in a circle to get the most leverage. She hadn't the strength he had, and she was going to need to put her whole body behind it if she was going to land the knife deep enough into his throat.

But she didn't land the knife into his throat.

He grabbed her wrist and twisted it until the knife fell from her hand.

With his other hand he grabbed her neck.

She looked at his face, curled up, knotted and twisted into a crooked visage of anger.

She couldn't breathe.

He was choking her and she couldn't breathe.

Her grip on Boy loosened and she began to lose the energy to struggle.

# CHAPTER THIRTY

Boy's HANDS hung onto her waist like she could fly away at any moment.

He didn't want to look at Dalton.

No, didn't want to look at him.

Too scary.

His face was strange.

Different.

*Don't want to look...*

He rested his forehead against Rosy's back. Felt tears in his eyes wetting her top.

Stupid tears.

Pathetic tears.

Too old for tears.

*I just don't understand...*

That was what the tears were about, after all. Not the fear, not the sight of Dalton's demented features, not concern for his safety – but incomprehension.

He wished he could understand these things, know why people looked or acted a certain way, but he couldn't, he couldn't, he just couldn't.

And that's why he wanted to cry.

Because Dalton had taken care of him. Found him a chess set. Played with him. Listened to Boy recite all the names of the different trees. Smiled at him, looked warm and inviting, like he could trust him, always trust him.

Now he was shaking and holding a knife and looking scary and looking angry and why was he so angry?

And why was he being so nasty to Rosy?

Rosy never deserved unkindness.

She was the nicest person in the world.

Her fingers stuck into his wrists and it hurt but it was okay. Even though she was squeezing too tightly and he could feel his muscles move back and forth under the tightness it was fine, it was okay, because she was doing it because she was Rosy.

Rosy always took care of him.

She let go of his wrists with one of her hands.

Why was she doing that?

*Please don't let go of me...*

Why was she lifting her arm up?

She took a knife from the back of her belt.

A knife.

She swung her arm and Dalton grabbed it and the knife fell to the floor and Boy just wanted to shut down and shut it all out.

Then Dalton's hands were on Rosy's throat.

And she took her other hand off Boy.

She wasn't touching him at all now.

Why?

He no longer felt protected.

*Please, Rosy, please let me know it's okay.*

But it wasn't okay.

He heard her spluttering, heard her choking, she couldn't

breathe, couldn't breathe, why couldn't she breathe, why couldn't she...

Dalton's hand was around her neck and he was looking into her with fiery eyes and he looked so mad but he was hurting her he was...

He was...

He was killing her...

He was killing Rosy.

He grabbed hold of her body, tried to yank on her arm to make her pay attention but it was going limp, going limp and empty and her body was shrinking and was she dying?

No...

*Rosy...*

He wanted to shut down wanted to crawl into a ball into a little tiny little ball where he could be oblivious to everything where Rosy wasn't being hurt where Dalton didn't look so scary where the world would shrink and everything would go away.

But he was losing Rosy.

Dalton was hurting her.

Boy saw the knife on the floor.

He picked it up and screamed.

*No one hurts Rosy.*

He swung it at Dalton but he didn't swing it well. He didn't try and aim or anything he just swung, hoping that Rosy would be okay.

As he dropped the knife he saw that he had scraped Dalton's leg, there was a small line of red with a little bit of blood creeping out.

But it was enough, because he let go of Rosy's throat and she sucked in air and she was okay.

Rosy was okay.

She grabbed hold of Boy's hand and dragged him forward,

pulling him, and he let her, because her hand was around his and her hand was warm and clammy but that was okay because it just meant that she was alive and they ran.

Boy looked over his shoulder and saw Dalton coming out of the doors but they were already across the field running and running and running and wow did his legs ache but that was fine he just kept running because Rosy was with him.

Rosy was there.

And that meant he would be safe.

Rosy always looked after him.

# CHAPTER THIRTY-ONE

CIA RAN FASTER than she'd ever run from any Thoral, or Maskete, or Waster.

This was worse than a Waster.

A Waster's instinct was the same as any animal instinct; feed and mate.

Dalton's instinct was...

*Stop thinking.*

She had to concentrate on running. She could over-analyse later.

Boy had just done an incredible thing, but again – she could tell him that when they were free.

She glanced over her shoulder.

Dalton was running after them. Crossing the field from the barn. She couldn't tell if he was gaining on them or not.

He took his gun from over his shoulder and tried to steady it.

The shelter of trees and bushes was getting closer, but not close enough.

She glanced back again. Dalton was still sprinting, just as they were, and he was aiming his gun as he did.

"Boy, listen," she said between gasps for air, not realising how much she was panting. "We need to run in zigzags, do you understand what that means?"

He looked back blankly.

"So from one side to the next, no sense to the direction you're running, okay? Like this."

She began zigzagging her runs, running from one side to the other, doing so without coherence or order – just sporadically placed steps that gave no clear target for Dalton.

"Follow me, Boy, come on!"

He did the same, and he did it just as she had asked. She was so proud.

The bullets came.

"Ignore the sounds!" Cia shouted, trying to be louder than the gunfire. "Just keep doing this!"

He did, as did she, and she saw the tufts of grass blow up behind their feet, but they were doing enough, creating enough chaos with their disordered direction to make them too difficult to aim at.

They reached the trees and Cia clutched Boy's hand, guiding him through, jumping over twigs and logs.

She glanced back and saw Dalton return his gun over his shoulder. He entered the trees and hit his shin into a wayward tree trunk, flying onto his front.

He stood, muddied and disgruntled, and Cia turned back to Boy, smiling at him reassuringly.

They were gaining distance. They were getting further away.

"Just a little further," she told Boy.

Another glance showed Dalton's silhouette disappearing into the distance.

His state of mind had gone. She didn't know him anymore. His madness was fuelling his rage, but it was also fuelling his recklessness. This wouldn't last long, she knew, he was a good fighter because of his instinct – but his immediate hostility was granting them enough luck that they could almost escape his sight.

They ran a little further, then a little further still.

Then they began to slow.

Boy was wheezing. He was trying so hard, powering forward, but he was struggling, and she knew his body wouldn't physically allow him to go on running much further.

Ahead she saw a fallen tree trunk, thick, branches surrounding it.

If they could get under that...

She came to a stop, as did Boy. She bowed over and placed her hands on her knees, unable to breathe fast enough for her lungs.

Boy mimicked her and did the same.

Gunshots rang out in the distance.

Now, it seemed, he was just firing anywhere in hope his bullets would find a target.

She put her hands on Boy's shoulders, looking him in the eyes as she always did when she had to request another action that may save their lives.

"We're going to get under this tree trunk and be as quiet as we possibly can, okay?"

He nodded.

"You understand, as quietly as we can?"

He nodded again.

"Good, come on."

She took his hand and guided him to the floor. She slid with him across the ground, mud decorating their clothes.

When they were finally under the tree trunk, coated in darkness, completely hidden in the soft ground that sunk under their weight, she put her arms around Boy and held him close.

She felt Boy crying into her top, but crying silently.

She stroked his hair, kissed his forehead. Told him it would be okay even though she had no idea whether it would be.

Heavy footsteps eventually approached, accompanied by gunshots and wayward shouting.

As they grew louder, some of the words became clearer.

"You can't hide, Cia!"

"You can't run!"

"I'll get him!"

"I'll tear his lungs out and make you watch!"

"I will rip his little fucking body apart!"

She kept her arms wrapped around Boy's head so he couldn't pick up the words, holding tightly and stifling his tears.

Eventually, the gunshots, the shouts and the footsteps passed.

They stayed there. Didn't move.

You never move straight away – rule number one to survival.

You wait longer than you need to.

Give it hours until you are sure that the predator has gone.

And that was exactly what they did.

THEN

# CHAPTER THIRTY-TWO

It DIDN'T TAKE LONG for Brooklyn to return to his typical, bolshy self. He walked with a limp for a few weeks after returning from the segregation unit, but that never dampened his spirits. The bruises faded, the cuts scabbed over, and the scars that remained stayed well hidden.

Not long after, they were circling the perimeter once more. Dalton was inwardly grateful for Brooklyn's company again, with his temporary replacement having been deadly serious and dead-faced. Brooklyn was annoying as hell and barely shut up, but at least that meant they didn't have to bullshit with small talk or incur any awkward silences.

"I tell you, mate," Brooklyn was yapping on, "We should be on it. Those birds in there have little to choose from, it increases our odds."

Dalton scoffed. He resented the term *birds.* He'd been raised by a strong woman and two older sisters who he knew would be throwing their arms in the air at such a term. But, whilst he didn't partake in Brooklyn's horny diatribe, he still found it somewhat amusing.

"I mean there are, what, a hundred single women, and

even more single men, yeah – but most of them are dirty, boring-as-shit politicians. They got nothing on us."

Dalton laughed.

"Boring-as-shit?" he repeated back with a chuckle.

"Yes, mate, I stand by my wise words – boring. As. Shit."

"Well you get on that. I'm interested to see how it goes."

"What about you?"

Dalton hit a twig and mentally scolded himself for not paying attention.

"What about me?"

Brooklyn placed an irritating arm around Dalton's shoulders. "I worry about you! All alone on all those nights... Sure there's nobody that takes your fancy?"

Dalton laughed at the suggestion.

"Hey, look, a guy's got to eat," Brooklyn continued. "And hey, we're in there with all those American birds – they got to love our sexy British accents."

"Our sexy British accents?"

"Shit yeah, bruv!"

"Bruv? You sound like Danny Dyer reading a crap thesaurus."

Brooklyn fell into hysterics. He dropped to his knees, buckling under the laughter, unable to steady himself under the weight of the hilarity.

"All right, all right," Dalton said. "Weren't that funny."

"Man, you don't joke much but when you do it's gold."

Dalton grabbed Brooklyn's arm and tried to help him up, but the laughter started again and he fell back to his knees.

Something caught Dalton's attention. He tried to ignore the laughter and identify what it was – a faint voice, small and timid.

"Hello?"

"Brooklyn," Dalton said, shaking him.

"What?" Brooklyn said, finally managing to stand.

They both looked to the source of the voice, where they found a boy, perhaps early teens, malnourished, standing a few trees across from them, alone.

"Hello?" Dalton said.

The boy looked to be on the verge of tears.

"What's your name?"

The boy didn't answer.

"My name is Dalton, this is Brooklyn." Brooklyn raised a hand. "What do we call you?"

"David."

"David. That's a nice name. Are you alone, David?"

David shook his head.

"Who are you with?"

"I was with my mum and my dad, but...I don't know where they've gone."

Dalton looked to Brooklyn, feeling a stare. He saw Brooklyn's eyes, and there was something about them he didn't like. Something inappropriately fun. He tried to ignore it.

"Would you like to come with us? We can help you."

David nodded.

Dalton waved him over and David approached.

"Where do you think my mum and dad are?" David asked.

"Be fucked if we know," Brooklyn interjected before Dalton could say anything.

"Brooklyn, man," Dalton said, shooting him a frown.

Brooklyn returned with a wink. That sneaky smile still there. Dalton realised Brooklyn was in one of those moods – he wished to toy with the boy.

Dalton really hoped he was wrong.

"Come on, we'll help you–"

"They are probably dead, to be fair," Brooklyn said again, sniggering.

"Brooklyn, mate, shut up," Dalton shouted. "What is wrong with you?"

Brooklyn shrugged. Still grinning.

Dalton lifted his radio to his mouth, waving David over.

"Central, come in, this is Dalton," he said.

The radio burst a second of static, then a voice spoke. "We hear you, go on."

"We found a life out here, a boy. Says he lost his parents. Requesting permission to bring in."

"What's his condition?"

Dalton dropped the radio and looked at David. He didn't seem to have any visible scars.

"You hurt, David?" he asked.

David shook his head.

"You sure?" Dalton asked.

David nodded.

Brooklyn raised his gun and pointed it at David's head. David jumped back, startled.

"Strip," Brooklyn demanded.

"What the fuck are you doing?"

"We have to be sure," Brooklyn told Dalton. "I ain't letting in anything that may have a bite, that's how shit spreads." He turned back to David. "Strip."

"Don't listen to him," Dalton urged the child. "You don't have to–"

Brooklyn cocked his gun.

"Do it."

David looked to Dalton, searching for the answers, looking for confirmation as to what he should do.

"No visible injuries on head, neck or hands," Dalton said into the radio.

"What about the rest of the body?" the voice on the radio asked.

Dalton dropped his head. Sighed. If they were going to help this boy, they were going to have to know.

Dalton turned and walked away, leaving Brooklyn to do the part that he was unwilling to do.

NOW

# CHAPTER THIRTY-THREE

CATHRYN STARED OUT THE WINDOW, always longing. Doing what she was told. Staying put.

Staying put, but worrying.

She always missed Daddy. She understood why he had to go out, why he had to leave the confines of the small home they had made in their small flat, but she still resented it.

She didn't used to. But after what happened to her mummy and...

She bowed her head. Covered her face. No more tears.

Daddy didn't mind the tears. She'd seen his tears too, especially when he thought she wasn't looking. Sometimes, at night, when she should be fast asleep, she'd hear them, a soft melody creeping into her room.

She didn't mind.

She liked that her daddy cried. It meant she didn't feel bad about crying too.

Peering out the window, she began to grow concerned. The sun was beginning to set, and she couldn't see any sign of him.

Was this the day he was going to leave her too?

No. *He'd never leave me.*

Then she saw something.

Well, someone. Two someones. Leaving the clearing by the trees. Emerging from the forest and into the street. A girl. A boy. He was taller than her, but he looked younger. Maybe more like her age, possibly a little older.

People always made her scared.

Daddy had always said – *run from the monsters, flee from the humans.*

He said to be wary of people in the world we live in now. That not all people can be trusted. But they looked trustworthy.

A distant screech made her shiver.

Where was Daddy?

She hoped he would help these two. They looked nice. Not nasty like he said some people were.

A growl shook the building. A thud in the ground, growing bigger and bigger.

A Thoral was approaching. She knew it. She recognised the sound. She often sat at this window, watching them.

Daddy was still out there.

With the Thoral.

She saw the boy and the girl become alarmed.

They looked around themselves.

They didn't know where to go.

Then a bush rustled.

*Daddy...*

# CHAPTER THIRTY-FOUR

Darkness had begun to descend. The cool air had settled and early evening had arrived.

That was never good.

It had been years since Cia had allowed herself to explore in the dark. God knows what might be lurking in the darkness, hunting you, watching.

As it was, she had no choice.

She needed to find them somewhere to stay for the night, and she didn't have the time to assemble a shelter with twigs before pitch-black would be upon them.

She gripped Boy's hand, unwillingly dragging him. She understood how tired he was, how much his legs were weighing him down, because she was that tired too. They had awoken in the middle of the previous night and hadn't slept since. Tiredness was clawing at the inside of her skull and she was wary about how delayed her reactions may be, how slow she may be to respond to threats, or even notice them.

But they had no other choice but to persevere.

Eventually, they cleared the wooded area and entered a small town. She had been surprised to find it, but in all honesty, they had been walking for miles and miles and it made sense that they would leave the shelter of the trees at some point.

The advantage to this was that they could find an abandoned house to squat in.

The disadvantage was now that they no longer had the trees to hide them. The trees had kept them unseen from flying predators, kept them hidden from faraway prying eyes. Now they were exposed – but, hopefully, their exposure would be brief.

Just as she began looking around, inspecting the looted shops, boarded up houses, smashed windows, silent sounds and eerie images of homes once lived in, Boy became a dead weight. The arm she had hold of pulled away and he stood, his feet roots in the cement.

"Come on," she urged him.

"No," he said, shaking his head.

"Just a little bit further, Boy, I promise."

"You already said that!"

It was true, she had told him a that quite a few miles ago.

She looked around. The open air. The empty sky above.

She grew more cautious – something felt wrong.

Anything could pounce on them at any moment.

"See these houses around us? We are going to find one to stay in, okay? We just need to look a little further."

"Fine. I'll wait here."

"No, Boy, you need to come with me."

"No! You find a house, then I'll come."

She sighed. She felt his frustration and could hardly hold it against him. She was battling fatigue just as much as he was, and she wanted to throw her arms in the air and declare this a pointless voyage.

But she couldn't afford the luxury of annoyance.

They had to find somewhere to shelter for the night. They had to survive.

"Look, Boy, I know how awful this is, but I'm worried that–"

She stopped talking.

Interrupted by a small but menacing sound.

Something distant, but close.

She listened – stood still, taking in every sound, from the rustle of leaves to the wind through broken windows to the–

A growl. Echoing. The source of which Cia could not find but could not mistake.

She looked around. Never mind somewhere to stay for the night – they now needed somewhere to hide.

"Did you hear that?" Cia asked.

Boy nodded.

"That was a Thoral. We need to move."

As soon as the word *Thoral* was spoken, he shut down. He covered his ears, closed his eyes, and refused to let there be a Thoral.

Cia wanted to burst into tears but didn't.

She'd had enough.

One thing after another.

And it was always up to her. Her job to ensure their survival, to fight the monsters, fight Dalton, fight everything. It was always up to her to break Boy out of his distress and force him to move and save him and *how are we not dead yet?*

The growl again. Louder. Closer.

"Please, Boy."

She really didn't want to go through the ritual again. Go through all the steps to calm him down when, at any moment, a large beast could jump out and rip both of them in two.

She grabbed his arms and ripped them away. Shook his head until his eyes opened.

Everyone has a tether, and everyone has a point when they are at the end of it – then there was a place far beyond the end of that tether, and that was where you'd find Cia.

"This does not help!" she snapped, and instantly hated herself for it.

Everything was piling up.

Every held back tear, feeling of quelled anxiety, worried nights with little sleep – it had all turned into a big pile of anxiety, and that big pile had been hovering above her head for a while and now, finally, it had broken and fallen all over her.

"Right, now let's–" she said, desperately forcing herself to keep her cool.

But she was interrupted by two things:

The ground shaking beneath them and wobbling the surface, accompanied by the sight of a Thoral landing its feet upon the crooked road.

And a bush nearby that began to move, then began to talk.

# CHAPTER THIRTY-FIVE

Colin was just on his way back when he saw them.

He didn't like leaving his daughter for long. Even before the collapse of society, leaving a seven-year-old home alone was not good – now it could be disastrous. But, safe in the knowledge that she was safe in the flat, he'd decided to see if he could find any more food. Now, dark was beginning to settle, and his forty-three-year-old legs weren't what they once were.

But there was something about these people...

Maybe it was his nurturing, fatherly instincts that were kicking in. After all, they looked so young. She was petite, maybe late teens – and he was probably only a few years older than his dear Cathryn.

In fact, he was probably the same age David was when he...

He huffed.

Why did every damn thought need to go back to what he'd lost?

He prayed that he'd never forget the fallen, but he still

had the greatest gift his late wife had given him – his daughter. She needed his focus now.

He stayed in the bush. His camouflage, his coat of leaves, had always kept him hidden when something sinister came crawling or flying or running or slithering past. As long as he stayed hidden, they rarely noticed him.

After all, his flat was in the building behind him. He had little ground he needed to cover, and keys to keep these people out if need be.

But they didn't seem like bad people. If anything, they looked like they were running out of willpower. They were encased in mud, so much so he could barely see what the colour of their clothes was. His instinct was that they were good people.

The way she was talking to him could be seen as impatient, but was more likely to be desperate. And when a growl shook the air and he refused to move, yet she didn't leave him – that's when he knew he had found two people worth aiding.

"This does not help!" she snapped at the boy.

Her face broke. As if she hated herself for being nasty. As if she had suffered such mental torment that she couldn't help but break.

She needed someone to help them.

"Right, now let's–"

The earth trembled.

He had moved his head to look at the Thoral before the ground's seizure had even registered.

It was huge. Drooling blood like they always did. Massive like they always were.

It was walking toward them.

These people were not moving.

It hadn't seen them yet, but they hadn't long before it would.

She was looking around, urgently searching for respite; somewhere to hide, somewhere to run.

But you can't outrun a Thoral.

And he was sure that, in her face, even for just a little flicker, he saw her give up. Saw everything she was fighting for become pointless.

She came to terms with their inevitable demise. It had been a good ride, but it was over. Their lives had run their course.

That's when he spoke up.

"Hey!" he shouted in a loud whisper. "Hey, over here!"

They looked over, confused, unable to see where the voice was coming from.

He poked his hand out of the bush.

"Down here!"

Then they saw him.

"Follow me!" he said, getting to his feet and ushering them.

With a glance back at the Thoral slowly stalking its prey, they turned and moved.

Colin led them a few yards down the street, to a door to a large building. What was once a huge group of flats.

Empty, of course, except for the very small candlelight burning behind the curtains of a flat six floors up.

He unlocked the door, let them in, then pressed himself against the wall, out of sight, as did they.

The thudding steps of the Thoral grew close, and he held his breath. He watched them looking at him with widened eyes.

Then the steps passed, and he let his breath go.

He looked them both up and down.

Both of them filthy. Potentially wounded. Unmistakably hurt.

"Are you okay?" he asked.

They looked at each other, then solemnly nodded.

"Follow me," he said, and led them upstairs.

As they did, they all allowed themselves a long outward breath of freedom.

For they all thought they were safe.

They all thought they had escaped the Thoral.

And they had – but there was still another monster they hadn't escaped.

THE FLAT ITSELF was a peculiar surprise.

The sofa wasn't torn up with springs poking out. The wallpaper wasn't ripped off. The windows weren't smashed. The carpet wasn't skewed by broken floorboards, the front door not beaten down, and the smell not that of decay.

It was even warm. Cia couldn't believe that they had central heating, but it certainly felt like it.

Colin guided them into the living room, and they followed absently. Their bodies were moving statically, their eyes wide but distant, their minds so fatigued they were barely aware.

"My name is Colin," he introduced. "And this is my daughter, Cathryn."

A young girl smiled at them, ribbons in her long, brown hair, and wearing pyjamas far more immaculate than they could conceive. She was sat at a child's table colouring in. Cia recognised the outline of the figure she was colouring in. It was a character from a book she used to love. She struggled to recollect his name... Hagrid, or something.

Colin removed his camouflage. It was an impressive outfit; a full body suit covered in leaves that would allow him to blend in with any bush or thick area of forest. Just as well that they lived next to such an area.

Beneath his disguise was a pair of jeans and a polo shirt. The kind that Cia's father used to wear.

"Give me a moment," Colin said, and marched into a nearby room.

Cathryn smiled at both of them. Despite their faces of terror, she wasn't deterred in her endeavour to keep smiling.

"Hi," Cathryn said.

Cia smiled weakly.

"Hi," she managed, her voice rough and small.

"What are your names?"

"I'm Cia...this is...Boy."

"Hello, Cia. Hello, Boy."

Colin walked out with a pile of clothes in his hands. He placed some of them on a table next to Boy, and on the arm of a chair next to Cia.

"Cia and Boy," he repeated. "Lovely names."

He stood, smiling at them. Why were they both so smiley?

"These are some clothes for you. Please feel free to get rid of what you're wearing, they don't look like something that a washing machine could particularly handle."

A washing machine?

Did this guy actually have a washing machine?

"Whose clothes are they?" Cia asked, not sure why she was asking.

"That, er...that doesn't matter. They won't be needing them anymore."

He smiled again, this time a little more forced.

"If you would like to use the shower, then please do," he said.

"You have a shower?"

Colin grinned.

"Oh, yes."

And man, did he have a shower. It wasn't just a few trickling beads of water. It was an immensely satisfying power-shower – a beating of water that would drench her and clean everything away.

Cia was so used to cold lakes that she was almost hesitant about using it, like it was some kind of trap.

She wanted to ask how exactly how he had a shower, but those questions could come later.

She led Boy into the bathroom, where she turned the shower on, and felt the water until it reached the right amount of heat – just like her father used to do for her. She assumed Boy wouldn't want it too hot, so once it was warm, she beckoned him to take his clothes off.

He covered his body, too shy.

She smiled and undressed herself, showing him it was okay. She stepped into the shower and closed her eyes as she lifted her head back and felt the water drench her hair.

There was even soap and shampoo in the corner of the shower.

She waved Boy in and, reluctantly at first, he removed his clothes and joined her.

They were both filthy, and the water that trickled beside their feet had barely any water in it – it was mainly thick mud, marred with a tinge of blood. She ensured that Boy had cleaned himself thoroughly, that he took advantage of this commodity.

Then, she beckoned him out and told him to go get changed.

And she was left alone.

Standing beneath the shower head.

Not moving, not thinking – just standing. Letting the

water punch against her and cascade down her body in an angry waterfall.

She turned the heat up, then turned it up more, until it was burning her. Until every part of her naked flesh had turned red and begun to sting.

And there she stayed, a catatonic state overtaking her.

Letting the water beat her.

Letting the heat scald her.

Letting her skin be touched yet still feel nothing.

Then it all came flooding.

The love she felt for Dalton.

The betrayal on his face.

The vow to kill Boy in front of her.

The terror, the anxiety, the stress.

The look in his eyes the look in Boy's eyes the running the hiding the listening to the bullets the being chased by him by the one she loved the one she relied on relied on relied on so bad to keep her safe as she kept him safe and he was going to hurt Boy hurt Boy hurt Boy he was going to hurt Boy and *oh dear God he was going to hurt Boy...*

Tears came suddenly.

They fired out of her eyes quicker than the shower. Hit her knees and the floor and washed away with the mud down the drain.

She cried heavier, and heavier, and heavier still.

Everything she hadn't felt surfaced.

Every hidden emotion, every corner of her mind she hadn't allowed herself to access, every piece of fatigue she felt in her aching muscles.

Everything.

*Every damn thing.*

It fell out, cascaded out, forced itself out until she was a heaving mess amongst a room of steam.

Then, finally, once everything had all fallen out, she finished.

She turned off the shower, dried her eyes, and dried her body.

She paused.

And it was done.

# CHAPTER THIRTY-SEVEN

Cia emerged from the bathroom, dressed in the clothes she had been given; a pair of loose jeans, a blue and white striped t-shirt and an amber woollen jumper. She was also grateful for a new set of underwear, having been living between the same five pairs for a while now; even if the bra didn't quite fit.

Boy was sat with Cathryn, some crayons in his hand, blissfully colouring away. He was wearing a t-shirt and jeans a little too big for him, but good enough for him to be content. He liked things a little baggy anyway, he didn't like to be constricted.

It was nice for him to be with someone else who was young. He was probably a few years older than her, but he'd never been able to experience childhood; not properly anyway. A luxury such as colouring in seemed like such a nice thing for him to do, and the smile on his face told her that.

"Would you like a drink?" Colin asked from the doorway to the kitchen, a kettle in his hand.

"Yes, please."

"A cup of tea?"

She nodded. The last time she'd had a cup of tea it had been made by her father.

She followed him through to the kitchen, admiring the pristine setup they had.

"This is a really nice flat," she observed.

"I like to keep it clean. But, to be fair, what else do I have to do with my time?"

She nodded. It was a fair point.

He lit a fire on the stove with a lighter and boiled the kettle atop it. He popped two teabags into two mugs. Once he'd filled the water, he opened the cupboard, took out one of many cartons of long-life milk and topped the mugs up.

"This is incredible. How do you have such a place?"

"This was our home before it happened, and it's our home now," he explained. "There's no one else in the flat block, just us. We're quite high up, so we don't get spotted that easily. I guess you could say we're lucky."

She'd agree with him. She imagined there had been many, many people in a similar place that had died. Yet here they were, father and daughter – she figured there had to be at least one person who'd been lucky enough not to perish, and here he was.

"How do you have a shower?" she asked.

He handed her the cup of tea and she held it in both hands. She sipped on it. It tasted good. She'd missed that. A cup of tea used to make any problem go away.

"There's a boiler in the basement," Colin said. "I've set it all up."

"You've set it all up? How?"

"There is a river running past this house. After about a year of going without power or water, I figured we may as well make use of it."

"I just don't understand how–"

"It's what I used to do – repair boilers, and so forth. I set up a small turbine in the water, and that generates our power. It's not enough to power the entire building, but as it's just us here, it suits us well. And the hot water, that took me a little longer – I created a way for the lake to feed into one of the boilers. Again, not enough for more than just a flat or two, but..." He noticed her confused expression. "It's simple really, when you know what you're doing."

She nodded. Wasn't sure what to say. Sipped on her tea.

"You're welcome to stay," he said. "I mean, you can have the spare room here for the night, if you like. But, I mean, there are lots of other flats. I'm sure I can direct some hot water to one of those, if you wished to take a home."

She almost laughed. It just seemed preposterous. The thought of just moving into a flat, setting up home and having hot showers...

It seemed like something they shouldn't have.

Which was odd, because – why shouldn't they? If it was available, then why not?

It wasn't like they would have such a thing at the cost of other people.

"It's a lot to take in, I know," Colin said, seeing the trouble in her face. "And I imagine you've probably been through hell. You'd have had to, to survive this long. But we're stronger together, right?"

She didn't say anything. She didn't know whether that was true or not.

"Hey, feel free to sleep on it," he continued. "There's no rush. We can talk, share our stories when you're ready."

She nodded. Took another sip of her tea. God, it was good. So warm.

"I think I'll go to bed now," she said, slowly and coolly.

She drank down the last bit of tea and placed the mug on the side.

"Good night," Colin said. "Your bedroom is the one on the left."

She nodded and left.

"Boy," she said, as she walked through the living room. "Time for bed."

He didn't put up a fight. She could see by his eyes how tired he was. She was surprised he'd stayed awake for so long.

They made their way into the bedroom where two single beds were ready for them.

They slept in the same one, her arm around Boy, holding him close, like she always did.

Once Colin had said goodnight to Cathryn, he decided to go to bed too. He blew out all the candles then retired to his bedroom.

At least, he thought he had blown out all of the candles.

But there was still one single, solitary, rogue flame dancing by the window...

# CHAPTER THIRTY-EIGHT

DESPITE THE COMFORT and warmth and blissful scent of the bed she found herself in, it kept her awake.

She wasn't used to it.

Every time she woke up slightly, as one often does throughout a night's sleep, she would panic and wake herself up fully. She would wonder where the bumps in the ground were, the wetness, the shivering cold – and she would look around, demanding to know where she was.

Then she would see that she was safe and settle back down.

Then again, was she safe?

She recalled the last two sets of people who took her in.

The first, a cult that demanded each woman be continuously fornicated with until they bore a child.

The second, a set of elitist survivors who originally denied her entry due to her skin colour, who had insisted that she instead be separated from her all-too-willing father.

Was she right to be cautious?

I mean, didn't this seem too good to be true?

She tried to unstiffen her body. Tried to let her head sink

into the pillow, its puffiness encasing her. Tried to let her body relax, wary of how much it was sweating beneath this heavy duvet.

It's strange what a person can become used to when forced.

She would normally be awake listening for sounds. Or, if not her, Dalton. On watch. Ready in case something caught them beneath the shelter they had created.

The trees normally disguised them well, as did the twigs she could straddle together to shelter them.

The noises outside of this building, however, were unlike the noises she heard amongst nature. It seemed that, without the protection of trees and guidance of wildlife, the quantity of monsters grew greater.

It seemed as if, any time she went to fall into a deeper slumber, she was woken by another screech or growl or thud or tremble or hiss.

She was attuned to them.

Her mind had been conditioned to wake up and become alert upon the sound.

She struggled to feel secure in her safety but willed herself to get some sleep. Who knew how long something like this could last?

Boy was fast asleep. Breathing heavily, eyes fluttering, snuggled beneath her arm wrapped tightly around him.

Among all the clean linen, she could really smell him. His sweaty stink. His grubby body giving off years of fear in one surprising odour. It was the kind of smell a dozen showers would still struggle to get off. And, before she could begin to feel repulsed by it, she grew starkly aware that she probably smelt the same herself.

On the bedside table was an alarm clock. Powered by batteries, she presumed.

It seemed a bizarre contraption.

To her, time had ceased to exist. There was the position of the sun in the sky and that was that. After all, time was a manmade invention. There was no forward and backwards, it was a concept created to measure events. Once people and events had all but gone, there was no need for time to exist any longer.

Yet they still had it.

She wondered if they knew the date, too. She would be intrigued to know what month it was.

The time itself read 3.46 a.m.

Was that late or early? She couldn't remember...

What was her bedtime when she still lived with...Dad.

*It still feels strange to think of him in such a way.*

To call him dad... It seemed undeserved.

*Daniel.*

Yes, she'd call him Daniel. That was his name, after all.

She tried to recall what her bedtime was when she lived with Daniel.

Eight, maybe? Half eight? Maybe nine?

Well, she was up far past it now.

She tried to sleep, but of course, when someone actually *tries* to sleep, it only reduces the chances of sleep and increases the chances of frustration.

So she stopped trying.

She listened to the sounds that seemed both close and distant.

A dozen or so Masketes were screeching, but she had to really listen to hear them, and she felt safe in the comfort that they were far away.

Of course, the deadliest predator was one she wouldn't hear coming.

But that was okay.

There was no way Dalton could find them.

Why would he think to look in a flat block?

No. She was safe.

She had to be.

As was Boy. Precious Boy, asleep beneath her arm. He was in such a deep rest, yet, she knew if she so much as took her arm away he would wake up.

She let her body sink into the bed, falling further into it, until she was engulfed by its pleasant warmth.

At some point she fell asleep, completely unaware of the threat that was approaching the building.

# CHAPTER THIRTY-NINE

Their tracks weren't tough to follow.

They had been sloppy. It was practically like leaving a trail of breadcrumbs. Boy's big feet and Cia's tiny feet had left a long line of footprints in the mud, guiding him seamlessly in their direction.

Dalton couldn't believe he'd been stupid enough not to search out their hiding place. That he'd naively kept following in same the direction, just aimlessly shooting in the hope of tagging one of them.

He'd been reckless. Foolish.

And whilst he swore it wouldn't happen again, he could feel his mind throbbing, could see his vision constantly refocusing, and he wondered whether he was thinking clearly.

It was dark but he wasn't tired. It didn't deter him. With the trees hanging over him, he was disguised. He could barely see in front of himself, but he didn't need to. His torch showed him the prints in the mud, the remnants of her running.

She'd been running from a lot of things, he figured.

The truth.

Her comeuppance.

The lies.

*She deserves to suffer.*

Whatever he could do to her would barely match what she'd done to him.

Not just him.

To a lot of people.

Her father. His friends.

Every single damn person in that damn bunker had died because of her. Yes, some managed to make it out, but how long would they have survived? How long would an inept politician who'd spent their entire lives being protected last in the real world?

Screeches sung above him.

Growls shook some faraway world.

Fuck them.

*Let them eat me.*

With way he was feeling, and with the rage that pumped through his body, he was ready to take on anyone, and anything.

Which was foolish, again. Reckless.

He wasn't invincible.

The trees grew sparser. The bushes began to thin. The sound of wind through leaves and branches lessened.

He was coming to the end of the woods.

This worried him. He didn't want to leave the protection of the trees. He hadn't expected Cia to, and he was going to have to think soundly and clearly about this.

He followed the footsteps further, until the trees ended, and a clearing revealed itself.

Beyond this clearing was a town. Abandoned, looted, broken down. Houses covered in moss, cracks in the ground, blood stained on the inside of shop windows.

The tracks ended as the mud ended.

He had nowhere else to follow them.

He wanted to punch out. Kick something. Shoot something.

But he reminded himself once more that he was not to be reckless.

Cia had lived long enough to show that she wasn't an idiot.

Violent. Sadistic. A liar.

But no idiot.

Just as his anger came to fruition, his annoyance at losing the tracks – he saw something.

High up in a flat block just across the street.

It was faint, but definite. A small light most likely lit by a single candle. A soft, barely noticeable amber glow against a curtain.

A growl shook the ground and he backed away from the street, reversed back into the clearing, into the darkness and shelter of the trees.

A Thoral came thudding past.

It wasn't safe yet.

But he knew there was a light. He was sure of it.

It had to be them. *It had to be.*

He was going to have to run.

He wouldn't see Masketes coming from the clouds, or Thorals from the darkness down the street, or Wasters bursting around a corner.

This truly was as pitch-black and pitch-black could get.

He checked his ammunition. Full.

He checked his knife. Tucked neatly in his belt.

He peered up at the window. Stared at it, as if willing something to happen, willing Cia to reveal herself, to peer out at the world below and show him that she wasn't as nimble and adept as he gave her credit for. That she wasn't smart, but just a sick, twisted little bitch.

He couldn't wait.

Couldn't wait to grab Boy's throat.

To tear him apart as that twisted little bitch watched.

He couldn't wait.

All he had to do was follow that candle.

THEN

# CHAPTER FORTY

Dalton found himself unknowingly staring at Brooklyn as he scoffed down his dinner.

This guy was his best friend, no doubt about that. He would do anything for him.

In fact, he had done anything for him – including taking a good beating from their sergeant and being locked in segregation for weeks because of it.

This guy was always on his side.

So why was Dalton beginning to grow scared of him?

What was it about him that was unnerving him so much?

His behaviour, it just...seemed to be becoming more and more erratic. Impulsively and needlessly hostile.

That kid...

Brooklyn was a bully. The child was probably terrified after losing his family in a world not made for solitary youngsters – and Brooklyn had taken advantage of that.

"What?" Brooklyn grunted, a mouthful of beans dribbling down his chin.

Dalton realised he'd been staring for a while.

"Nothing," Dalton said, looking down and returning to his own selection of fried items. He absently prodded at a piece of bacon, pulling at the fat.

"Nah, what is it?" Brooklyn insisted. "You were staring at me for ages. I know I'm pretty, but I ain't that pretty."

"I don't know. I was just...thinking. Forgotten what it was I was thinking about now."

Dalton could feel Brooklyn's stare now on him, lingering, shovelling a mouthful of bacon and sausage into his gob.

"It's the kid, ain't it?" Brooklyn asked.

Dalton sighed. He didn't want to get into this. Brooklyn wasn't the easiest person to engage with when it came to his views on other people and the world they now lived in.

"Come on," Brooklyn persisted. "Spit it out. You got beef, share that beef."

"It was just–" He stopped himself. He really didn't want to do this. "That kid, man. He was so young."

"Weren't that young."

"Couldn't have been older than ten."

"At ten years old I was beating my step-dad with his own belt for beating on my mother. Ten ain't that young."

This was exactly what he expected. Stubbornness confronting him like a tank speeding head-on.

"Forget it," Dalton said.

"Nah, come on. I want to know what made me such an arsehole with this kid."

Dalton placed his cutlery down. Turned fully to Brooklyn. If Brooklyn was as good a mate as Dalton thought, then Brooklyn would be willing to listen to him.

"What if that kid had family?" Dalton said.

"Okay," Brooklyn said, still shovelling his food down. "What if he did?"

"Wouldn't it be good of us to help him get back to that family? You know, instead of teasing him while he's scared."

"I didn't realise we were such a bunch of do-gooders."

"You don't have to be a do-gooder to do the right thing."

"The right thing?"

Brooklyn put his cutlery down too. Took a long, drawn-out gulp of beer. His face twisted like it did when he was readying himself for another one of 'Brooklyn's life lessons for the insane.'

"What does that even mean?" he asked.

"What does what mean?" Dalton retorted.

"The right thing. What is 'the right thing'?"

"The right thing is helping others, is taking care of a vulnerable child, is–"

"Nah, see, you're coming up with what the right thing was *once*. You know, once upon a time where we still lived in a society that went beyond an underground bunker. You're talking about the morals of a world that no longer exists."

"You don't need society around to know that it's wrong to be nasty to a poor child."

"That's a point of view. Like right or wrong, which is also a point of view. And is the point of view of people still in the hangover of a world destroyed."

He swigged down another few large gulps of beer.

"Brooklyn–"

"No, Dalton, you listen to me. I love you, man, you are my brother – but you keep your beliefs to yourself, and I'll keep mine to me."

Brooklyn took his knife and fork in his fists and resumed diving into his sausage, shovelling it into his mouth with the juices squeezing out of his lips.

"Let me just ask you one more thing," Dalton said. "What about his family?"

"Don't give a fuck about his family."

"Imagine they showed up. They didn't like how you treated their kid. They wanted to do something about it. What then?"

"What d'you mean, what then?"

"I mean, say they really didn't like it. Say they threatened your life. What would you do?"

Brooklyn shrugged.

"Kill 'em."

He finished the last of his bacon and threw his cutlery onto his plate with a loud clatter.

"You would kill them?"

"I would kill anyone who threatened my life. Or yours."

"Come on, you wouldn't–"

"Listen to me, Dalton," he said, jabbing his fat finger across the table, ignoring the faces that were beginning to turn toward him. "It's the world we live in now. No one's stopping them trying to kill me, same as no one's stopping me trying to kill them."

"You really feel like that?"

"If there's one thing I can teach you about this new haven we find ourselves in, Dalton, it is this – if someone hurts you, kill them."

Dalton stared back at Brooklyn, not sure what to say.

"Kill them, and kill them dead, Dalton. If they don't deserve their life. Snatch it away from them. You got to be willing to kill to survive in this world. Kill, or you'll never make it."

Brooklyn stood, picking up his tray and walking away.

Dalton watched him go.

He didn't feel like eating the rest of his meal.

Brooklyn's words kept repeating around his mind.

*You got to be willing to kill to survive in this world.*
Was that really true?
Brooklyn seemed to believe it.
*Kill,* he had said.
*Kill, or you'll never make it.*

NOW

Dalton had been trained by the army. Therefore, he was confident that he knew all he needed to know.

He was a soldier.

He was an expert in stealth and combat. He could craft a masterpiece of death. He was the Leonardo da Vinci of war.

But, as magnificent a painter as Leonardo da Vinci was – if you were to feed his mind nothing but anger and wrath, then all his paintings would become a chaotic mess.

And Dalton's crafted masterpiece was soon becoming just that – a chaotic mess.

His hellish fever fed off his lust for vengeance and impaired those abilities he had spent so long honing.

Even his footsteps were loud. His body barging into the doorway as he entered the sixth floor, his gun clattering in an echo around the corridor as he collapsed to his knees.

He wiped his sweaty brow.

Pushed himself up with wobbling muscles.

He'd forgotten which window they were at. He'd counted, but the information had since faded.

But he didn't need to remember.

He saw a faint amber glow seeping from beneath the crack of a door a mere few yards away.

He knocked into the wall, drunk without alcohol, ecstatic without ecstasy – and reminded himself of the need for stealth.

He turned the handle.

Locked.

No matter.

He put his gun over his back and withdrew his knife, squeezing it into the lock, and jimmying it until it opened.

The door slowly and silently swung open, displaying a room lit by a single candle.

An empty room.

Dalton rubbed his eyes. Willed his vision to focus.

As silently as he could step, and as catastrophically clumsy as he couldn't fight, he edged into the room.

He stood. Still. Listening. Sensing.

From a nearby door came a soft snore.

He'd recognise that snore anywhere. He'd had to sleep beside that snore for months. Sometimes it kept him awake, and sometimes he was so tired he could drown it out.

Boy's snore had never bothered him before.

Now it *incensed* him.

He edged toward the door, knocking his knee into the sofa and cursing the instant pain of a stricken knee cap.

Slowly, he rotated the handle and pushed the door ajar, revealing a darkened room with a bed in the far corner. A duvet – the luxury of the few – wrapped around a sleeping body, that same snore still humming away.

He couldn't wait to end that sound.

And this was it. What he wanted. To end Boy's life as a way of destroying Cia's. The beginning of his vengeance – it was still not enough compared to what she had taken from him; but it was a start. One life lost to begin to make up for the thousands she took.

He kept his knife out, edging, softly placing his feet to avoid the moan of the floorboards.

He walked into the end of the bed and tripped, falling to his knees, and hastily looked up to see if he'd awoken the beast.

Nothing.

As unaware of the world in his sleep as he was when he was awake.

He stood over him.

A lump entirely concealed by the duvet.

The heavy snores of the innocent.

*Innocent.*

Dalton decided he shouldn't think such a word.

No one who had survived could be innocent. No one could have survived this long without committing horrific acts.

He retracted his knife.

Threw it downwards, into the side, relishing the swift sound of its slice, feeling the soft squidge into the flesh.

He pulled his knife out and swung it downwards again, prompting a yelp.

That must have woken him.

The damned snoring had ended.

He stabbed again.

And again.

And again.

Then, seeing the body turn over, making out the shape of Boy beneath the covers, he could see where the throat was.

He plunged the knife downwards, sticking it in and

holding it there, watching the duvet dampen, thicken with blood, growing in a pool across the cheap material.

There was a scream.

And Dalton took his knife out, watching the soaking blood grow at a far higher rate.

# CHAPTER FORTY-TWO

Cia's eyes opened with an urgency she was too sleepy to comprehend.

It took a few seconds to grow alert and realise what had awoken her.

Was that a scream?

As if answering her thought, it came again – though this scream sounded concealed. A deep, guttural scream, full of gargles.

Cia checked for Boy next her.

There he was, beneath her arm, eyes shut.

She shook him.

He didn't wake.

She shook him harder, and eventually his eyes opened.

"Boy," she whispered, "don't make a sound."

A commotion came from the adjoining room.

"We need to go," she told him.

"But I'm sleepy..." he objected.

"I know, but it's not safe, there's someone in the other room."

"No, I want to sleep!"

A clatter. A smash.

There was something there.

How long until it found them?

"Boy, get up," she said, and pushed until he fell out of bed.

He went to moan and object, but Cia didn't give him the chance – she stood, putting a finger on his lips and listening intently, straining to hear what was happening through the random sounds.

"Get your bag," she demanded, finding hers on the floor and pulling it over her shoulders.

Boy delayed, as if deciding whether to be cooperative or angry – so she didn't give him a choice. She grabbed his bag and shoved it over his shoulders.

She took his hand and opened the door, peering out.

The commotion was happening in the bedroom next to hers – the bedroom between them and the door.

The door was open.

Cia paused, considering their options.

They could run and hope that whatever it was didn't give chase.

They could creep and hope not to be noticed.

They could wait and see what it was, see whether they could fight.

"Daddy?" came a quiet voice emerging from the bedroom to the other side of theirs.

Cathryn walked out, rubbing her eyes, inquisitive, meandering toward her father's bedroom.

"Cathryn!" Cia said in a shouted whisper. "Cathryn, stop!"

Cathryn looked at Cia, as if deciding whether to stop, whether to trust her. She frowned, scowling at this new stranger, and decided she needed her father's protection.

She ran to her father's room.

"No, Cathryn, no!" Cia urged.

Cathryn ignored her, entering the doorway to the room with all the vile sounds.

Cia stepped out, still clutching Boy with one hand, reaching out to Cathryn with the other.

Then Cia saw him.

Her eyes locked on his.

And her whole world came shattering down.

# CHAPTER FORTY-THREE



Those screams were too…

Manly.

Too grown up.

Dalton flung the cover back – and there, staring up at him, were the wide eyes of a middle-aged man. Throat covered in blood. Eyes empty of life. An unknown corpse – a body that meant nothing to Dalton.

"*Damnit!*" Dalton cried out.

He turned around, not knowing why – just feeling a stare, feeling something watching him.

A little girl.

Maybe this guy's daughter.

Staring at him.

Just staring.

She didn't cry. Didn't scream. Didn't run, advance, fight, make a sound – just stared at Dalton.

That was, until she saw Daddy.

Not moving. Covered in blood, just like her mummy, just like her brother…

She screamed.

Dalton went to move, then saw something that rendered him immobile.

From behind the girl, he saw her.

Clutching onto Boy.

Wearing pyjamas. Fancy silk pyjamas.

He wasn't sure why, but this enraged him more.

He had been outside, fighting his fatigue, fending against the weather – and she was in here, warm, tucked up beneath a duvet, wearing pyjamas.

His lip curled into a snarl.

His snarl grew into a growl.

And his growl grew into a spurt of energy that powered his charge forward.

The little girl turned and ran.

"Cathryn!" Cia cried, but she was too late – the girl left the flat and the quick patter of her steps disappeared down the corridor.

Cia made her choice between fight and flight quickly and instinctively, taking her knife from the side pocket of her bag and holding it out to Dalton.

He didn't care.

He grabbed her throat in his giant paw and squeezed, relishing the sight of her face turning red, the spluttering of her chokes, the panic in her eyes.

"Don't worry," he told her. "I'm not going to kill you until you've seen me tear your precious Boy apart..."

Dalton's threat turned her panicked splutters into anger-powered resilience. She threw her arm downwards, sticking her knife into the chunky flesh of his thigh.

He cried out and momentarily loosened his grip, thus allowing Cia to escape it. She took her knife from his thigh, grabbed Boy and ran.

It was okay. His cry was just instinct. It was barely a graze.

She hadn't hit anything important. She couldn't. She didn't have the strength.

He pushed himself up and ran, battering into the wall of the bedroom, to the door frame, to the corridor where he fell to his knees.

*Get a grip.*

He needed to wake up, break his funk, get some resemblance of sense.

They turned to the stairs.

He charged after them, bashing into one wall to another, and ran to the stairs.

He tried to leap down four at a time, but his heel slipped, and he skidded down the steps. He took to his feet and carried on running downwards, head first, in a constant state of falling, barging into the railing, grabbing it with his sweaty palm, the only thing that kept him steady.

They were a few flights down.

That was fine.

He'd get them.

He knew he would.

# CHAPTER FORTY-FOUR

Cia left the safety of the flat block; their home that could have been.

Realistically, it was never going to work. They were never going to be able to make a life there.

Things like that didn't exist anymore.

Running water.

Duvets.

Pyjamas.

She felt ridiculous for even entertaining the notion.

They were doomed to face the outdoors forever, to embrace the horrendous weather and constant threat of monsters.

As if to confirm this, she heard a deep Thoral growl shake the distance as she emerged from the block.

She let go of Boy and sprinted, knowing he would do the same. She kept a few paces ahead of him, hoping that would encourage him to keep up.

Dalton gained on them with ease.

She aimed for the clearing, but they didn't make it there in time.

She had no choice.

He dove onto her legs, taking her to the floor – but she was prepared. She turned and mounted him, holding her knife above in the air.

She looked down at his face, and it almost destroyed her; a brief, drawn-out second where she saw what he had become.

Pale. Bags under eyes. Helplessly perspiring. Shaking – trembling, almost.

Had she done this to him?

Quelling the thought, she reminded herself that he was a threat, and she needed to eliminate that threat.

She took the knife in one hand, grabbed his head with the other, and exposed his neck.

Boy waited a few steps behind her. Watching.

She was never more aware of him watching than she was at that moment.

She didn't want to do this in front of him. This wasn't like killing a monster. This was a human, even if there was little human left in him.

Would this change the way Boy saw her?

Would he be scared of her?

Would this make her a different person – at least, through his eyes?

She'd killed before. To get back to him, to save him; she'd killed.

But never while he stared at her.

She couldn't think any longer. She had to act, then deal with it later.

She swung her knife down to Dalton's throat.

It stopped less than an inch from his Adam's apple.

And there, it hovered.

Poised.

Shaking.

Just a push, a bit of muscle, a little prod, and it would be in.

But she couldn't do that push, that bit of muscle, that prod.

She couldn't.

Everything Dalton was came lurching up like a mouthful of sick. Not just the person he'd been, but the idea of him – the notion that she could fall in love and be happy in a world designed for them to perish.

Pushing that knife another inch would end that completely. Would destroy any idea of the life they had tried to create.

She knew there was nothing of that life left, that sparing him would not allow anything to go back to how it was.

But she couldn't.

She just...couldn't.

She bowed her head. So disappointed with herself.

*I can't...*

She moved her knife away from his throat.

He laughed.

"You can't do it... You coward, you can't do it..."

He was right.

She'd had the opportunity to end this threat, to cease his chasing – but she couldn't let her arm move that extra inch his death would require.

His laugh turned to a cackle, which turned to hysteria.

Fine, she couldn't kill him.

But she could still run.

She leapt to her feet, grabbed Boy's hand and took him as far away as she could manage.

It didn't take long before she could feel Dalton gaining on them once more.

# CHAPTER FORTY-FIVE

THE UPPER HAND was surely with him now.

She couldn't do it.

She could destroy a Sanctity of thousands, but just him, this one individual person – she couldn't.

She was still clinging onto something.

He laughed as he ran, knowing she could hear him.

He didn't need to run fast to keep pace.

He hung slightly behind, to taunt her, to know there was no chance of escaping.

He was faster. Better.

And he was going to do what she couldn't.

No, actually, he wasn't.

*I'm going to do far worse.*

# CHAPTER FORTY-SIX

SHE RECOGNISED THE FOOTSTEPS, chasing, running. The same heavy stomps she'd heard any time running had been involved in the past few months.

She wiped her eyes.

No time for tears now.

Then she realised, she wasn't upset. She was angry. Fuming. Raging at herself.

Why hadn't she killed him?

She'd had her knife by his throat. Ready to end this. End the threat to her and to Boy.

And he'd laughed at her.

The bastard had laughed.

Mocked her for not having the gumption to kill a man she thought she loved.

She hated herself. She was such a fool. Such an idiot.

All she had to do was push the knife another inch.

He had no way to stop her. And all she'd have to do was push that knife.

An inch, that was it.

*Just an inch...*

It would have done it...

He was gaining on them. She looked over her shoulder. He was almost in reach.

She grabbed hold of Boy's arm and pushed them further, sprinted harder, put more energy into their limited supply.

And to think, an hour ago she was in a bed. Thinking that was how life could be. Thinking that there was a way for them to move forward in life without all the running and chasing and...

God, stop it.

*Stop it!*

This wasn't a time for overthinking or over-analysis.

A clearing in the trees was coming closer. She didn't recognise it. She hadn't been to this part of the forest before.

A stream of wind hit her.

It was a cliff edge.

She pulled a loose log down and watched as it tripped Dalton. This gave her a few seconds.

They reached the cliff edge and came to a stop.

She looked below.

A devastating drop.

Then water.

The best luck of an unlucky situation. They could fall and survive. They could dive and splash and fall deeper, then she could open her eyes and swim Boy back to shore.

She looked over her shoulder.

Dalton emerged, slowing to a walk.

Approaching.

Knowing she had nowhere else to go.

"We're going to have to jump," she told Boy.

He shook his head with as much vigour as his weary body would allow.

"I know," Cia said. "I know, Boy. I know it's tough. But this is the only way."

She glanced back over her shoulder.

"Dalton is going to hurt us," she told him. "But if we jump into the river, we'll be fine."

"I can't swim…"

"That's okay, Boy, I swear, that's okay. I'll find you. The moment we hit the water, I'll find you. I won't let you drown, I promise. I would never let you drown."

She looked back at Dalton. He was grinning lecherously. So happy with himself.

"When I get to one," she told him. "Three."

She looked down and her legs felt weak.

But she hid it.

Couldn't let Boy see.

She had to show him nothing but strength.

"Two."

She gripped his arm. Even if he didn't jump, if he was too scared, too unable – she was going to make him. She would be grabbing hold of him, making sure she took him with her.

She put a second hand on his arm to make sure.

"One."

She leapt.

Boy went with her.

But she didn't fall. She found herself hanging. Dangling over the edge, clinging onto Boy's arm, who was somehow still on land.

Behind Boy was Dalton, holding on to his leg.

"Let him go!" she screamed.

Dalton lifted his knife and reached it downwards. He didn't care if he fell, didn't care what he did or what happened to him – all he seemed to care about was keeping Boy from her.

"Please!" she begged.

It was no good.

Dalton lifted the knife and swung it downwards at Cia's arm.

Cia kept her grip on Boy, which allowed the knife to dig into her forearm.

Her grip loosened.

And she let go.

And she fell.

Watching Dalton and Boy disappear into tiny figures.

She screamed, bellowed, lit her lungs on fire with her anguish.

She fell into the water, far, far below the cliff edge, and far, far below Boy.

She kept sinking under.

Alone.

Without him.

Completely without him.

THEN

## CHAPTER FORTY-SEVEN

Jacey wasn't the same kind of company as Brooklyn. In fact, she was startlingly quiet. Dalton was ashamed to admit to himself that, without Brooklyn's constant, arrogant boasting, he found himself feeling quite unsettled.

But he'd needed a break.

Brooklyn was loyal and strong, but he was also foolish and stubborn. He was set in his beliefs, of which he was aggressively passionate about, and sometimes it could get a bit much.

But he wished Jacey would talk.

He watched her walk a few paces ahead, gun in her hand, looking around, sticking to the perimeter like there was a line she was following. Being vigilant in a way Brooklyn never was. Her shaved head and baggy combat trousers epitomised the image of the army, but it was an image Dalton had always found himself uncomfortable with.

He wasn't the laddish bloke a lot of his friends were.

Which was another thing that made his friendship with Brooklyn all the more bizarre.

"Who do you normally pair with?" Dalton asked, not really caring but wanting to end the silence.

"What?" she asked, turning around.

"I said, who do you normally pair with?"

"Oh. Mikey, sometimes. Luke. Occasionally Swade."

"Oh." Dalton nodded. He had no idea who any of these people were.

"What about you?"

"Normally Brooklyn. There's only one time I been out without him before, and that was when he was in seg."

"Brooklyn, huh?"

Her reaction made him regret bringing Brooklyn up. It was the same reaction people always seemed to give to the mention of his name.

"He's not the dick you all think he is."

"I'm sure he's not. I just ain't seen a side of him that isn't a dick as yet."

Dalton huffed.

Should he bother getting into this discussion?

How did it always end?

With him running out of argument and the other party always convinced that they'd persuaded Dalton of Brooklyn's idiocy.

"He likes to create an image," Dalton said, reluctantly being drawn in. "He likes to show off. Make everyone think he's a big man. But he's not. Not really."

"What's he really like then?" she asked, looking around at all times, gun ready for anything. So unlike what he was used to.

"He's loyal."

"Loyal? That it?"

"Funny."

"Nah, he just thinks he's funny."

"And he's…"

What?

What was he?

What else could he say that was good?

"He would always have your back in a scrap. I guarantee, one of those creatures attacked while he was with me, he'd put himself between me and it."

Jacey forced a smile.

"Sure you're not seeing him how you want to see him?"

"What do you mean by that?"

"I just mean… I don't know anyone else who would say this."

"You just don't know anyone else who's his friend."

"Doesn't that say something as well?"

Dalton sighed. Just as he'd expected, he'd been cornered into a debate he couldn't find his way out of. The same arguments, the same response, and him with a lack of things to say.

Maybe Brooklyn was a dick.

Maybe they were all right.

Or maybe he was right, and they just didn't know him.

Or maybe no one was right. Maybe they just believed what they believed, as did Brooklyn.

"Look," Jacey said, sensing his discomfort. "I'm glad you got a friend in him. In this world, we need all the friends we can get. And if you've got someone who would lay down and die for you, then, hey, who am I to argue with that?"

They paused a moment. Looking at each other. Somehow, she made him feel a lot better.

"Thanks," he said.

"No problem, after all–"

She stopped talking. Her eyebrows narrowed. She looked perplexed, like she spotted something.

"What is it?" Dalton asked, trying to peer at what she'd seen.

"What the hell is that?"

She rushed through the leaves, between the trees, and Dalton followed.

Eventually, she came to a foot.

A child's foot. Small. Unintentionally exposed.

"What is this?" she asked.

Dalton felt sick.

He feared the worst, then grew angry with himself for doing so.

Jacey kicked a bunch of leaves, revealing the body that the foot was attached to.

She kicked all the leaves off.

A young boy stared back at them, no life behind his face. A dead, pale corpse left hidden beneath the leaves.

"Why would one of the creatures hide a kid's body beneath the leaves?" Jacey mused, crouching beside the body, searching it.

Dalton went to answer, but didn't.

Because he knew a creature wouldn't hide the body beneath leaves.

Only a person would do that.

She lifted the boy's body, turning it onto its side, to reveal a thin slice across the back of the boy's neck.

Across the back of *David's* neck.

"This was done by a knife," Jacey said, growing confused.

"Are you sure?" Dalton asked.

Of course she was sure.

He just didn't want her to be sure.

After all, anyone could have done this.

Any survivor could have traipsed by, happily going about their business, and...

And what?

Just killed a kid for no reason and left his body to rot?

"No creature did this," Jacey said. "A person did. Who would have done this?"

Dalton kept his mouth shut.

He dreaded the thought, and he refused to acknowledge it to himself, but he was fairly certain he knew exactly who'd done it.

NOW

# CHAPTER FORTY-EIGHT

THE WATER WASHED Cia's body upon the shore, throwing her out of the lake like a discarded wrapper or piece of plastic.

She rolled onto her back. Groaning. Groggy. Staring at the sun punching back at her.

She rolled onto her front. Pushed herself to her knees. Her arms hurt from the impact of the fall, the smack of the water; as did her face, her neck and her ankles. Any part of her skin that was exposed. She felt heavy, her clothes thick with water, drenched to exhaustion.

She removed her top. Screwed it into a long thin line, twisted it, and rinsed it. Water collapsed and thudded against the bank. She rinsed it some more, until all the water was gone, and unwrapped it. It was still wet, still creased.

She took off her shoes, which were just as heavy.

She took off her trousers, rinsed them too then put them back on.

She carried her shoes in her hand as she trudged into the trees, making her way beneath their overarching twists and turns, the branches obscuring her from anything flying overhead.

Then she fell to her knees.

Deliberately, yet unintentionally.

And she finally let herself feel it.

*Boy.*

*Dalton.*

*Boy...*

Dalton had slit Colin's throat. Had killed him, right there and then. Something she never thought Dalton could do. Even in his terrible state, she never imagined him capable of killing an innocent man for no reason.

Was this her fault?

If she had never destroyed the Sanctity...

*Then things would be much worse.*

Her father would still be alive.

She fell to her knees. Not sure why, but finding herself suddenly incapable of walking. She rolled onto her back, sinking into the soil, wincing at a stray nettle scraping her arm.

*Boy...*

*Dalton...*

*Boy...*

Now Dalton had Boy.

If Boy was even still alive.

And she was far below them, far away, and no idea of where they were.

Dalton may well have slit Boy's throat just like he did that man's. Boy may well be lying dead beside Dalton's feet, glee across his face, manically happy at achieving his revenge on Cia.

But she didn't feel like that was right.

She remembered what Dalton said. His adamant intentions.

He wished to make Cia suffer. He wished to kill Boy in

front of her. He wanted Cia to witness Boy's torture. He wanted her there to see his agony, to feel it herself, before he turned on her.

Surely he wouldn't kill Boy yet, or harm him yet, because she wasn't there to witness it.

But if that was the case, where on earth would she find them? How would she willingly arrive to be his audience?

She closed her eyes.

Man, they were so tired.

Her eyelids met comfortably, feeling nice, feeling warm.

But she couldn't keep them closed.

She had to open them.

She had to find Boy.

But how? It was no good. He was lost.

She'd found him before…

And now she was without him again it was as if part of her body was missing. Like her side, or her leg wasn't there, and she was going to have to limp and struggle to find it and reattach it and–

She sat up.

"Oh my God," she gasped.

She knew where he was going.

At least, she had a pretty good idea.

But it couldn't be that simple.

Did she even know how to get there?

She leapt to her feet, almost giddy, before realising the hard part was still to come.

Still, this had potential.

She cast her mind back to a conversation she had, barely a week ago. When they were on their travels, toward the Sanctity, and they passed a cottage.

She recalled Dalton's words:

*If we get separated while we're down there, or if we get*

*separated any other time, then that cottage will be our rendezvous. That's where I will meet you.*

The farm they had passed. The dainty little cottage. The dream home.

That's where Dalton would be.

And that's where Boy would be.

# CHAPTER FORTY-NINE

Cia had to be prepared.

She couldn't just run in there, waving her arms about, beseeching Dalton's better side to surface.

She needed weapons.

Unfortunately, neither the river nor the woods were a place to find guns or knives. She'd had a large knife, but she couldn't find it anymore. It had probably floated far down stream by now. All she had left was a small blade tucked on the inside of her belt.

If something chose to attack, she was exposed. Completely and totally open and vulnerable to any creature that sought her out, any predator that decided she could be their meal.

But when it came to wrath, she had a heavy arsenal.

And she had an idea as to how she may acquire more weapons.

She trudged between trees, searching out the right one. Boy's recognition of all the different tree types had somehow sunk in, as she somehow found herself deliberately identifying the different trees, trying to find what she was after.

She came to a large trunk, surrounded by acorns.

She pulled down the branch and studied the leaves.

She recalled what Boy had said as he handled the branch of a tree not too long ago...

*Lobed, these leaves are lobed, rounded or pointed.*

She ran her thumb across the centre of a leaf. He was right. The leaf was rounded, extending out from its centre line.

She let the branch go and reached her hand out to the trunk, resting her hand on it, brushing her palm down gently, feeling the surface.

Small. Scaly. Just as Boy had said.

Surrounded by acorns.

*This is an oak tree.*

Then she recalled Dalton's words spoken so soon after Boy's, as he carved an arched piece of wood:

*It's best to use oak.*

She took her tiny blade out, grabbed the thickest branch she could reach with one hand, and sawed it from the tree with the other.

She began carving. Curving and scraping the blade, quickly, roughly but precisely. Remembering the image of Dalton doing it, and mimicking as exactly as she could.

She created a slightly curved stick of around four-foot in length, using her thumb to figure out the thickness. It wasn't done as easily as Dalton had managed. She'd had to use all the strength she could muster, running on pure adrenaline, but she created a bokken just like he had.

And, just as Dalton had, she rounded its end and narrowed it into a sharp point – then she made it sharper still.

She even rested her thumb on its tip so she could feel it prick, and watched a tiny blob of blood form in a bubble.

With the rough edge of a discarded piece of the tree, she sanded the surface of the bokken down, particularly focusing on its handle.

*The tsuka*, as Dalton had told her.

She paused.

Watched the Japanese sword she had somehow manufactured sit neatly in her hand.

What was she doing?

What was she planning to do? Just go and stick the end of this into Dalton?

Stick the kissaki in – that's what Dalton had said the end was called.

How would she manage that?

She wouldn't even know how to create this if it weren't for him.

She lifted the wooden sword. Gripped it. Felt its weight. Spun it in a circle. Waved it to the side and back.

She could use this.

It could kill.

It could.

*Really...*

She allowed herself a deep breath.

Looked up at the hill she had to climb.

Thought about how much she hated this, how much she didn't want to do it.

Could she even stand a chance against Dalton?

She'd had her opportunity. She'd swung the knife to his throat.

And she'd stopped.

Her body had made her physically unable.

Just as she completely doubted herself and decided the venture was pointless, she pictured Boy's face.

Remembered all the nasty things Dalton had said he was going to do.

She took the first step.

And the next.

And the one after that.

And she kept stepping forward, climbing the hill, pushing herself against her body, ignoring the weight of her legs.

Until, eventually, she knew where she was, and she could begin the short ending to her voyage; to the cottage where she was certain she would find her two boys.

A GENTLE AUTUMN breeze attempted to turn the page of Boy's book.

He wouldn't have it.

He slammed the page back down, adamant that he would continue to read about the Maidenhair tree. He liked that one especially, partly because of its funny leaves, and partly because of its really funny name. Its leaves were shaped like clovers but silly, and its real name was actually Ginkgo Biloba, most known as Ginkgo.

What a stupid name.

He tried saying it aloud.

"Ginkgo."

He chuckled to himself.

"What's that?" Dalton asked, standing in the doorway to the cottage's kitchen. Boy peered across the garden surrounded by a picket fence, watching Dalton as he dried his hands.

"It's the name of a tree," Boy told him. "It's called…"

He couldn't say it. It was just too silly.

"It's called– it's called–" He stifled his chuckle. "A ginkgo."

Dalton smiled warmly.

"That is a funny name."

He stepped out into the garden. He stood next to the garden bench where he kept a selection of items that Boy was sure were parts of guns.

Boy hadn't wanted to sit on the bench. It wasn't comfortable enough. The ground, although slightly wet and splodgy, was far kinder to his rear-end than the hard, bumpy, splintering surface of the bench.

Boy watched, intrigued at what Dalton was doing. Dalton seemed to be taking all of those random parts, sticking them together, again and again.

There was one weapon that hadn't been taken apart. It was a knife. A smooth leather handle with a large curved blade. Dalton seemed to like that one the most. He was moving it back and forth, in front of his face, spinning it, ogling at it like it was supremely interesting, which was confusing, as it wasn't interesting. It was just a knife.

Dalton turned to Boy, noticing him staring.

"Like my knife, huh?"

Boy shrugged.

Like he'd thought, it was just a knife. He'd seen lots of them.

Dalton tucked the knife into the reverse of his trousers and sauntered over to Boy, where he crouched, still smiling, as if he was about to say something but was taking ages to say it.

"When's Rosy getting here?" Boy asked.

Dalton sighed.

"You said she was coming. That she was okay. That she would have survived the fall, and that she would know to meet here."

"She would have, and she will."

"So when is she getting here?"

"You really want her to get here, do you?"

"Yes! Of course I do!"

Dalton sighed again, this time bigger, like he was demonstrating something, but Boy couldn't tell what. He could never figure out why people kept making strong outward breaths, but he knew that some meaning was meant to be attached to them.

"I don't think you do want Rosy to get here," Dalton said, in that tone of voice one has when about to deliver grave news. "I really don't."

"Of course I do."

"But I don't think you understand what's going to happen when she does get here. To her. To you."

"Why? What's going to happen?"

Dalton stopped crouching. Stood up and stretched. Held his arms out. Then he sat down on his knees.

"Right now, me and you, we're friends, aren't we?"

Boy shrugged. "I guess."

"I think we are. I think we've been very good friends. Don't you?"

"Yes."

Boy couldn't understand Dalton's tone of voice. It seemed condescending yet sinister. Why would that be? Why would he be talking like that?

Boy felt like covering his eyes. Covering his ears. Screaming.

But then he wouldn't see Rosy coming.

Far away, a Thoral growled. Dalton didn't flinch.

"Because, when she arrives, you and I – we're not going to be friends anymore."

"Why?"

"Because I'm going to do some very, very bad things. Some very bad things, Boy, do you understand?"

"Not really."

"I am going to hurt you. And Cia – Rosy – but I'm going to hurt *you* first. Do you know why that is?"

Boy shook his head.

"Because I want Cia to watch. I want her to suffer by seeing you suffer. Do you understand?"

He shook his head. He really didn't.

"Cia did something very bad. To me. And to a lot of people. She is responsible for a lot of people's deaths, see. And for that, she has to pay. She has to suffer."

"Are you going to hurt Rosy?"

"Yes," he said smugly. "Yes, I am. But that part, I'm afraid, you won't be around to see."

Dalton stood. Stretched. Wiped his forehead on the back of his sleeve.

Boy tried to decipher Dalton's words. Like a code he had to break.

Dalton was talking about hurting him but he'd never hurt him.

Rosy had told him that.

She'd told him he could trust Dalton.

Dalton was still watching him. Casting Boy in his shadow.

"I'd like to say you'll understand some day," Dalton said. "But, unfortunately, you won't live to that day."

"I won't live?"

"Boy – which, by the way, is a fucking stupid thing that I have to call you – I am going to tie you up."

"Why are you going to tie me up?"

"Because then I'm going to violate you from the inside. Rip your skin open to reveal your disgusting guts. Then slit your throat while I force Cia to stare into your eyes. Has that made it clear enough?"

*Violate... What does violate mean...*

*Cut me from the inside...*

*Rip my skin...*

Dalton was still staring at him.

Boy went to close his eyes, went to cover his ears, when to moan and whine and scream and wish it all away, wait for it all to go away, wait for Rosy to show up and take his hands away and whisper to him and make it all okay.

Then, in the distance, he saw her. Her figure approaching. Limping and weak but approaching.

And, with her close by, he felt less afraid.

Then he saw Dalton turn. Saw Dalton look at her. Saw the look on his face.

And when he saw that look, he finally understood all of Dalton's words, and began mentally going through all the horrible things that were about to happen.

THEN

# CHAPTER FIFTY-ONE

Dalton watched her.

The girl from the outside.

The one everyone was talking about.

Small. Mixed-race. Bushy, curly hair.

But pretty. So damn pretty. The kind of pretty that would make your skin hairs stand upright, that would make your belly flutter, that would make your entire ability to form full, complete sentences falter and turn you to a wreck.

*That* kind of pretty.

She was unconscious. Dalton ran in with her, beside the bed, clearing the way, gun at hand. He wasn't sure what he was carrying his gun for, but he felt an overwhelming need to protect this girl – this *woman* – from any straying eyes.

They reached the lift and the doctor punched in floor 126 – the operating floor – then stood there tapping his toe, agitatedly waiting.

He was surprised they had let her in.

But then again, Dalton had known the guard on duty. The man outside the door. He knew that this man would not send someone away for the same reason as their imbecilic president or inept, sheepish prime minister would.

Her eyes twitched. A breath flicked a hair out of her face.

*Oh God...*

He needed to get a grip.

*It's like I've never seen a woman before...*

Maybe that's all it was. Used to the same faces for years, the same women who had either rejected him, not appealed to him, or had turned out to be immensely incompatible.

Maybe it's that he was impressed. For her to have survived for so long she'd have to be quite the person. Quick-witted. Quick-thinking. Sharp.

*Jesus, now I'm inventing her personality...*

The lift doors opened.

"Thank you, Private," said the doctor. "We can take it from here."

He stepped out of the lift and gave way, allowing them to push her down the corridor.

Brooklyn stepped out of a room as he did and managed to get a good look.

Dalton hated that Brooklyn saw her. Wasn't sure why. He just hadn't wanted Brooklyn to know about her. Like he didn't want the competition, or he wanted her to be his little secret.

Then he saw the look on Brooklyn's face and knew exactly why his knowledge of her existence gave him a sense of grave predicament.

Brooklyn's lips pursed as if to say, "phwoar!" He held this expression the whole time he walked up to Dalton, walking with a fake limp to... God knows why, trying to pretend to be gangster, or suave, maybe? Perhaps his idea of a joke.

"She's a pretty little pistol, isn't she?" Brooklyn declared.

Dalton said nothing.

"Where'd we find that one?" Brooklyn asked, a lecherous grin still smacked from cheek to cheek.

"I found her outside," Dalton said, his voice monotone, unimpressed. "She was unconscious."

"Well done you! I've never had a brown one before."

"She's not brown."

"Black, brown, green, whatever she is."

"By the look of her, I'd say she's of mixed heritage."

"What does that mean?"

Dalton shook his head and walked on. Brooklyn didn't seem to take the signal, and he followed.

"I mean," Brooklyn carried on, "I tell you, mate. The things I could do to a fancy little thing like that."

"What makes you think she'd want you to do those things?"

Dalton hated himself for getting drawn in. Reminded himself not to.

"How could she resist?"

"You're not God's gift to every woman out there, you know."

"Maybe I won't give her much choice."

Dalton stopped, forcing Brooklyn to stop. Brooklyn's face didn't match the anger shaking his. If anything, the smug look on Brooklyn's face only fuelled that anger more.

"What are you saying?" Dalton said. "You're going to force it on her?"

"Relax, Dalton. All I'm saying is we live in a different world now."

"A world where a woman doesn't have a choice?"

"Jesus Fucking Christ, mate, I was joking. Lighten up, would you? When are you off duty? I fancy a beer."

From sexual assault to a beer break in a matter of syllables.

That summed up Brooklyn.

"I'm not off duty for hours," Dalton lied. "Go on without me."

"Right you are, shit-face."

Brooklyn sauntered off, that fake swagger to his walk, that arrogant stride to his legs.

If only Dalton had known, right then, what was going to happen, he may not have spent the rest of the night worrying about it.

As it was, he couldn't seem to get this woman out of his mind.

NOW

# CHAPTER FIFTY-TWO

Cia saw them.

Dalton and Boy.

She saw them as she approached, unease stabbing at her chest.

What did she expect?

Dalton armed, firing at her, running at her with a knife?

Whatever she had imagined, it wasn't this: Dalton standing neatly over Boy, in the garden, watching her approach.

She slowed down. Gaining ground with caution. She pulled the wooden sword out and held it ready by her side, the sharp end as ruthless as the blade tucked into her belt.

He smiled as he saw her weapon.

"You are a good girl," Dalton said as soon as she was in earshot. "Taking the lessons I taught you. Look at that! It's got a point as prickly as your personality. What a beauty."

"I don't want to do this, Dalton," she said.

"Do what?"

She paused a few yards from the fence.

Dalton walked casually to the garden bench where she

saw an array of weapons, some assembled some not, all ready and assigned to a different part of her torture.

"What is this?" she asked.

He really had lost it.

From a kind, caring human – to *this*.

"You're a monster," she quietly muttered.

"What?" Dalton said, patronisingly cupping his ear.

"I said you're a monster. You're no better than a bloody Lisker. Or a Thoral." Dalton began laughing. "Or a Waster, or a Maskete."

"Let me ask you a question – how many people have I killed?"

She shrugged.

"I mean, since you've known me – it's just been that guy, right?"

"You mean Colin," she stated bluntly.

"Oh, that his name? Don't really matter, question that I'm asking is, how many people do you know of that I've killed? So far, just the one, yeah?"

Cia shrugged again. She really didn't care, she just wanted this to end.

"And when I'm done with you and Boy, that will be three, right?"

"I guess," she said, waving her arms in the air. She turned her attention to Boy and began thinking how best to put herself between the two of them.

"And how many people have you killed since you've known me?"

"None."

"Wrong."

"Okay, one – my dad."

"Wrong again."

He cocked his gun.

He pointed it at Boy's head.

"Try again."

"I don't understand what–"

"How many people," Dalton demanded, his voice now impatient and shouting, "Have *you* killed?"

"Why don't you tell me?"

"Two thousand six hundred and thirty-three."

Cia stared at him. *He really has lost it.*

"What are you talking about?"

"That was the population of the Sanctity, Cia. That's how many people you killed."

Ah.

Now it all made sense.

"So there's no way I can talk you out of this?" Cia asked, resigned to the fate she once thought impossible.

He just gripped the gun he pointed at Boy, who sat there with leaves draped around his feet, his face concealed by his own quivering arms.

"Drop your weapon."

Cia looked back at him, weighing up her options.

She could drop it and they would both be exposed.

She could give it up, and Boy would live – for now.

Or...

What?

What else?

She had no choice.

The most important thing was survival and, for that reason, she threw her weapon to the floor – but she threw it beside Boy, in hope that he would find some way to use it or keep it for her.

"What now?" Cia asked.

"What do you mean, what now? Come and get what you came here for."

*Come and get what I came here for?*

He was talking about Boy. Boy, who had covered his ears and buried his face in his hands. Boy, who was shutting himself away from a world he couldn't handle.

"You came here for Boy, didn't you?" Dalton persisted.

"Yes," Cia said, still not quite understanding.

"Then come and get him."

Could it really be that simple?

"What's the trap, Dalton?"

"Trap?" he echoed, looking around inquisitively.

Whatever he was planning, at least this would put her between them. At least her body would protect Boy, for as long as Dalton would allow.

She stepped forward, climbed over the picket fence, and edged into the garden.

Keeping her eyes on Dalton's gun at all times.

She stepped another pace closer to Boy. He was in reaching distance now.

Dalton backed away to the bench. Put his gun down. Picked up his knife.

Why on earth would he do that?

Cia paused. Steps away from Boy, but sceptical.

Why would he back away and discard his gun for a knife?

"What have you got planned, Dalton?" she asked.

He smiled.

"Do you want the fucking kid or not?" he asked.

*Fine,* she decided.

She would put herself between them.

She stepped forward, went to the ground and put her arms around Boy. Stroked his hair, kissed his forehead, spoke to him as softly as she could, "I'm here, Boy, I'm here now, it's okay, it's okay."

She didn't see what Dalton did, but she heard the swing

of his knife. He plunged it downwards, and she went flying into the air.

It took seconds for it to happen, then far longer for her to readjust.

She now dangled from a wayward tree branch by her ankle, right above Boy, looking down at him.

Boy, whose foot moved out of the leaves surrounding him to reveal a rope around his ankle.

There was something Dalton had slashed, some kind of rope that led something buried in the leaves, something that now had her helplessly flailing in the air...

She thrashed and fought, but this only made her swing and felt nauseous.

Dalton stepped forward with his large, curved blade and stood over Boy.

"You really are a fucking idiot," he stated, clearly and concisely.

He grabbed Boy by the hair and dragged him as far across the garden as the rope around his ankle would allow, before pressing him face down in the soil and mounting him.

With his knife, he cut through Boy's shirt and scraped a line of blood down his back. Boy screamed like he never had before, wailing that was so much more than the whining he often did.

A Maskete screech responded.

Dalton looked over his shoulder at Cia and grinned.

She dangled there helplessly, forced to watch.

Forced to watch, as she moved her hands upward, behind her back, reaching for the blade tucked inside her belt.

# CHAPTER FIFTY-THREE

She wasn't subtle about it.

No need to be, really.

There was no discrete way for her to find herself out of this predicament.

She waited until Dalton's back was to her, until all that could be heard were the heart-wrenching wails of the person she wished to protect more than anyone else in the world.

She swung up and grabbed the rope around her ankles with one hand, took the blade from her belt with the other, and sawed through the rope. She dragged her blade back and forth, until it frayed and grew weak, twisting her arm until it ached.

She ignored Boy's cries.

They were killing her, but she had to think clearly and strategically if she wanted to prevent any more of his tears.

"What are you doing?" Dalton shouted.

By the time he had stood up and charged at her with his blade, she had cut the last bit of rope and fallen on her back. She cried out as she felt something hurt, but ignored it.

Dalton swung the knife for her, but she managed to roll away from his swipe and leap to her feet.

There they stood. Opposite each other. Looking into each other's eyes, each with a blade in their hand, awaiting the other's move.

Circling.

Watching.

Waiting.

She clutched the blade.

The wooden sword was a few paces behind him.

He snarled. Took a few small steps as if he was readying himself. Clutched his weapon tighter, stiffening, getting ready to pounce.

He was stronger than her. Quicker. Better. Trained by the army. All she knew about such combat was what he had taught her.

But, as it turned out, that would be enough.

He lunged for her.

*Duck, duck, swing* – that's what he'd said, and that's what she did.

She ducked the first swing that went over her head.

Ducked the next that went down to her left.

And swung her blade into the side of his ribs.

Took it out quickly, not long enough for him to recover from the pain, and stuck the blade into the wrist that held his knife, forcing his palm to open and the knife to drop.

She went to her knees and stuck her blade into his right foot.

Took his knife and stuck it into his left foot.

Punched both blades in further, and further still, so that they stuck through his feet and into the ground, holding him firmly in place.

He collapsed to his knees, screaming and wriggling and prodding at the sharp edges stuck in his feet. He tried pulling at one to release it, but this only caused him to cry out in further anguish.

She took a few more steps, picked up the bokken and returned.

She took his right hand in her left, stuck the bokken through his palm and wedged his hand into the ground. He fought with his one free hand, only to find it too painful to move.

Boy was in the corner of the garden. Shaking. Staring. Immovable.

Cia went to him and crouched. Rested her hand on his face, but only momentarily. She wasn't ready to see to him yet.

She untied the rope from Boy's ankle and threw it at Dalton, who was still crying. Writhing. Pulling at the blades with his one free hand; the blades that were too sore to pull out, and too fixed in place to remove without the strength he no longer had.

Blood had become him. Trickling into the leaves, sinking into the ground

He collapsed, delirious, losing energy and losing it quickly.

But still alive.

Cia took Boy's hand, stroked his face, and rested her forehead on his, speaking as softly as she could.

"Boy, it's okay," she said. "I've stopped him. No one's going to hurt you now."

He looked at her.

She placed her hand on his back and he winced.

She led him into the cottage, where she found a broken

wooden chair and sat him on it. She took some of the leaves and began dabbing at his wound – it was the best she could find.

The whole time she did this, she kept her eyes on Dalton, making sure that he neither moved nor stopped suffering.

# THEN

# CHAPTER FIFTY-FOUR

*Evacuation, get to first floor.*

*Evacuation, get to first floor.*

Dalton reacted to the rude awakening with a rub of his eyes. He'd only just managed to start dozing. Now what?

He rolled out of his bed, threw his feet on the floor, and looked to the top bunk where he'd expect to see Brooklyn.

He wasn't there.

The click of a gun being assembled drew his attention. Behind the bed, he saw Brooklyn.

"Brooklyn?" he asked, his mind quickly readjusting to being awake, and his voice drowned out amongst the urgent instructions.

*Evacuation, get to first floor.*

*Evacuation, get to first floor.*

Thudding pounded outside the room. He opened the door to find all the other soldiers moving from their rooms, running across the corridor. The emergency message was even louder in the third floor corridor.

He shut the door and searched for some paracetamol.

"Brooklyn!" he shouted. "What's going on?"

Brooklyn turned to him, a machine gun held across his chest, a look on his face he hadn't seen before; something between alarm and excitement.

"What are you doing?" Dalton asked, unnerved by this look.

"Have you not heard?" Brooklyn said.

*Evacuation, get to first floor.*

*Evacuation, get to first floor.*

"No, what's going on?" Dalton shouted, cupping his ears.

"The creatures on the bottom level are loose. They've gotten out. Everyone is evacuating."

*What?*

How the hell could they get out?

They were pumped full of depressants, chained up with an excessive amount of chains, forced into submission. They had been so for years, how could they possibly be out now?

Brooklyn rushed to do the door.

"Wait then, mate," Dalton said. "I'll come with you."

"Negative," Brooklyn replied, somewhat distracted.

"What are you on about? I'll just be a second. We can go to the first floor together."

Dalton dressed as quickly as he could, tied his boot laces, and searched for his gun.

"I'm not going to the first floor," Brooklyn announced.

*Evacuation, get to first floor.*

*Evacuation, get to first floor.*

"What are you on about? Of course we're going to the first floor!"

"Nah, you are. So's everyone else. I ain't."

"Where the hell else are you going?"

Dalton looked at Brooklyn with utter confusion, complete mayhem dancing in his mind.

Then he realised.

It dawned on him.

And it all made sense.

And, in that moment, more than any other, he learnt who Brooklyn truly was.

His friend, but a friend who was only constricted by morals that were forced upon him.

"Don't be an idiot," Dalton said. "You can't seriously be thinking of–"

"Listen." Brooklyn stepped strangely close to Dalton, and Dalton grew instantly wary of Brooklyn's gun. "I haven't had a nice piece of ass for ages. It's been fucking years, you hear me? Now I get the opportunity, with no one telling me no."

"I'm pretty sure she'll tell you no."

"I'm pretty sure it won't make a bit of difference."

Brooklyn turned to leave, but Dalton grabbed his arm back.

"So you're going to what? Find her, fuck her and die down there?"

"I don't care about this shitty little existence, Dalton. Look around! What have we got? Nothing! I just..."

"Don't do this–"

"I am fed up of living by the standards of a society that don't exist no more."

Brooklyn turned to leave again, but Dalton grabbed his arm once more.

"What!" Brooklyn screamed, lowering his gun with a tight grip.

Dalton stared at it. To Brooklyn, to the gun, to Brooklyn.

"She's seventeen, mate," Dalton said.

"Old enough for me."

"Don't be that guy."

"What guy? Shut the fuck up, Dalton, with your righteous

shitty chat. What, you want to convince me? Tell me what's right or wrong? Go to hell."

Brooklyn went to leave. Dalton grabbed his arm once more, and this time, Brooklyn raised the gun to Dalton's face.

The thudding steps from outside had left.

The army would no doubt be getting ready to escort the richest and most powerful inhabitants of the Sanctity out.

Isn't that the way it always goes?

"I can't let you do this," Dalton said.

"What you going to do?"

"I don't know. I don't... know. I just... I can't let you."

"Let me ask you a question, Dalton – are you willing to die for this girl?"

Dalton didn't answer.

Just looked back at the eyes behind the gun.

Brooklyn turned and left the room.

This time, Dalton didn't pull him back.

He let Brooklyn walk out.

And he stood there.

A fool.

Maybe Brooklyn was right. The world had changed. Baser instincts come into play and there's nothing he can do about it.

He could leave. Get to the first floor. Beat the creatures.

He was sure that's where Joe would be heading. He could find Joe, find his way out.

He could *survive*.

Without another thought, he made his decision.

He grabbed his gun from beneath the bed and walked out into the hallway.

Brooklyn was charging down it, almost at the end.

Dalton took aim. Fired. Waited. Fired again.

Brooklyn grabbed his spine and fell to the floor.

Dalton ran over to Brooklyn's writhing body and kicked his gun away.

He pointed his gun at Brooklyn's head, Brooklyn's face staring back up at him, entwined with betrayal and anger.

"You bast–"

Dalton shot again, Brooklyn cutting himself off, expecting it to end.

But Dalton was out of ammunition. He hadn't reloaded, and he'd left it in his room.

Brooklyn laughed.

Dalton dropped his gun and went to his knees.

Looked at his friend.

Placed his hands around his friend's throat and applied as much pressure as he could. Squeezing, pushing down, putting all the weight of his body upon his grip.

It took longer than he thought it would.

After ten seconds or so, Brooklyn began to splutter. He tried lifting his arms, but the gunshots in his back must have severed his nervous system or something, as he struggled to even twitch.

Brooklyn's eyes emptied, but Dalton knew that didn't mean he was dead yet. That just meant he was unconscious.

So he kept going.

He heard footsteps. Heavy. A lot of them.

People were coming.

But Dalton kept going.

Kept going until he could feel no breath from Brooklyn's mouth against his arm. Until, eventually, Brooklyn's face was still and empty, and he finally let his grip go.

He stood and looked at Brooklyn.

*Please evacuate to the first floor.*

*Please evacuate to the first floor.*

*Please evacuate to the first floor.*

More people appeared and ran, a horde of them barging past him, and he stood, in the middle of the floor, watching people run past him in streams of chaos, listening to the loud woman's voice that didn't shut up and just clogged his thoughts.

*Please evacuate to the first floor.*

Why bother rescuing Cia? Would she bother rescuing him?

Or was this just because he had a crush on her?

Hell, it couldn't just be a crush. Look at what he'd done for her.

"Fuck it," he muttered.

She may not have known it at the time, but, in that moment, it seemed that Cia may have been his only friend.

NOW

## CHAPTER FIFTY-FIVE

THE SILENCE inside the cottage was bombarded by the growing noise out of it.

Dalton screaming. Agony taking over. Cries where he pleaded for help and cries where he told her she was a bitch were all intertwined with cries that were indecipherable.

Behind all that noise was screeching. Masketes, no doubt about it.

They were far away, but they were definitely approaching.

She finished drying the large cut across Boy's back. She was worried it would get infected. Leaves hadn't done that great a job at cleaning the wound.

She opened the cupboards of the kitchen, but nothing but dust blew back at her. She flinched and wiped her face. There was nothing here.

Glancing at Dalton, and assuming he wasn't going anywhere, she took Boy's hand and led him into the bathroom.

She tried the taps, not quite sure what she was expecting

to happen. Nothing came out. There wasn't even any water in the toilet.

Maybe this wouldn't have been quite as nice a place for her and Dalton to live as she had thought.

Funny that, how something can seem so great on the surface, but once you go in and look around, it turns out to be a useless, broken down shack.

She could still hear Dalton. Clear as if she was stood right next to him.

She sighed. She was going to have to deal with that before she dealt with Boy's wound. Before the Masketes arrived.

She sat Boy down, took his hands in hers and crouched before him. Looking him in the eyes.

Those sweet, blue eyes.

He looked hurt. Not just physically, but like his trust had been battered. Like he'd experienced something that would change him, and she wasn't sure exactly how it may change him and she dreaded to think of it, but she knew he needed her now more than ever.

Taking both of his hands in hers, she brought them to her lips and kissed them. Closed her eyes. Held them there, tightly. She felt the urge to cry and fought it.

Not yet.

"I love you, Boy," she said. "I love you more than anything in this world. You know that, right?"

He nodded.

"No, really – you know that?"

"Yes, Rosy."

"I would do anything for you. Including..."

*Killing for you.*

She didn't say it, but she thought it.

"I'm going to need you to do one thing for me, okay?"

He nodded.

"You've been so, so brave so far. And I'm sorry that you're hurt – and I will see to your wound, I promise. But, like I said, I just need you to do one thing for me. Yes?"

He nodded again. A big nod.

"I need you to wait here for me."

"No, don't go away!" he yelped.

She closed her eyes. Bowed her head. How could she explain this to him?

Dalton's screaming bombarded her thoughts.

"Please, Boy, I just need you to be brave. I'll be...minutes. If that. Okay?"

She took one of her hands from his and put it against his cheek.

"I'm going to shut this door. And I need you to close your eyes and cover your ears. Okay?"

He nodded.

"Do it for me now, please."

He closed his eyes. Covered his ears.

"The devil has departed," she said, against the hand cupping his ear. "And you are not alone."

She stood.

"Take time to rebuild, Your love in our home."

"Shared time it is slowing," Boy said, taking over. "The pace of our heart."

She stepped out of the bathroom.

"But from now to the end, We won't be apart."

She looked back at him.

"The devil has departed," he began again. "And you are not alone."

She shut the door.

She could still hear him, but faintly.

A cold absence took over as she contemplated what she was about to do.

Then she stopped thinking about it and listened to Dalton's screams, incessantly declaring that she was a bitch, a traitor, a whore.

She stepped outside.

Took the knife.

And took the last few steps to the gallows, until she was by his side.

"I *HATE* you!" Dalton screamed.

He was flat out on the floor. Even the one hand that was still free was beginning to lose its feeling. He felt himself sticking to the ground with his blood, his cheek against it, his mouth moving with the last few bits of energy he had.

"You bitch! You traitor! You whore!"

He heard her step outside.

He heard the slide of back door, followed by her final steps toward him.

"I trusted you! You killed everyone I knew, and I trusted you! I would have died for you!"

Her feet crossed his vision and paused. He tried lifting his head to look at her better, to see her face, to see her evil bastardised face one more time.

But his neck wouldn't move.

So he had to make do with her feet.

"You..." he continued, battering his verbal tirade against the ground with what energy he had left. "You fucking... you... you evil, conniving... bitch..."

A head rush clouded his mind. The world began to spin. His vision obscured by colours.

He grew dazed.

Distant.

He saw her knees. She must be crouching.

He felt cold, yet warm at the same time. Warm in the places he was wounded, cold everywhere else.

*Is this what it's like to die?*

"You little... little..." He struggled to find the words, yet he still searched for them. "You wicked, evil... evil... you... I hate... I hate... you..."

"Please," he heard Cia's voice say. Not shouting, growling, or anything like that – just gentle. Like he remembered her voice being back at the beginning. "Please, Dalton. Don't make me do this."

"Do what... You backstabbing... backsta... back... back..."

"I don't want to do this. I really don't."

"Fucking do it! I dare you! I dare... I..."

"Why did it have to be this way?"

*Why?*

How dare she ask that...

How dare...

He tried to shout that at her.

*How dare you ask me that!*

*You did this!*

*You did this when you killed everyone!*

But words no longer formed. They came out in a breathless wheeze. A broken stutter.

The world grew distant.

Then he felt pressure. Her knees in his ribs.

Screeches.

Masketes were coming.

Maybe they'd get her...

Maybe they'd...

Maybe...

A flicker of light in metal shone before him, then the knife was at his throat.

He closed his eyes.

Felt the scrape.

It didn't work at first. She tried to slit his throat, but in real life, it's not that easy.

But she tried again.

This time, she managed. Blood drenched his chin in spurts, soaking him in its thick warmth.

He tried to breathe but he was already past that.

His eyes didn't close. He didn't let them.

They stayed open long after.

His final thoughts faded. His mind stopped attempting to form them.

Fairly soon, he was just a body, lying stiff in the floor.

The Masketes descended, picking at what was left; but by then Cia was gone, and he was just bird food, nothing else.

# CHAPTER FIFTY-SEVEN

"The devil has departed and you are not alone. The devil has departed and you are not alone. The devil has–"

Boy stopped speaking the poem.

He waited.

*She should be back by now.*

He didn't know how long it had been, or how long she had intended to be gone – but he knew it had been too long.

What if she was hurt?

She'd said that he needed to be brave.

Brave boys take their hands off their ears. Brave boys can listen to horrible things.

But there were no more horrible things.

Screeches, yes, but no more shouting. No more nonsensical outbursts of evil words.

He was brave. He took his hands from his ears and stood.

Walked to the door.

Put his ear against it and listened.

The screeches were really close now, but there was something else. It sounded like her, but it wasn't words. It was... sobbing. Gentle sobbing stifled by silence.

He opened the door and peered out.

At first, he jumped.

A group of Masketes were visible in the garden, across the corridor and through the kitchen. They were distracted, though. In a circle, picking at something. He couldn't see what, but they were having a good go at whatever it was.

But the other noise. It was coming from behind him.

He stepped into the corridor, watching the Masketes, sure that they wouldn't see him, and he walked away from them, toward the sobbing noise.

He entered what must have once been a living room but was now a vacant mess. Torn apart sofas covered in dust, a smashed television, a rotting carpet.

The sobbing was coming from the corner of the room, and that was where he found her. Huddled up. Her arms around her legs. Rocking. Hiding herself from the world.

Just like he often did.

When he couldn't bare the world, this was what he did.

So he thought... how did she help him when he was like this?

So he walked toward her. Slowly. Knelt. And placed his hands ever so gently upon her cheeks, and looked deep into her reddened, wet eyes.

"It's okay, Rosy," he said. "It's okay."

But the eyes looking back didn't look okay.

So he did what she did when he struggled to stop. When she didn't get him out of it so easily.

He sat next to her, tucked his arms around her, and held her close.

Kissed her forehead.

And said nothing.

Just sat there, with his arms around her, being close and being there.

Because that's what Rosy always did for him.
And that's what he would always do for her.

DAYS LATER

# CHAPTER FIFTY-EIGHT

CATHRYN KEPT RUNNING until she couldn't run anymore.

Daddy...

No...

He was so still. So stiff.

His eyes were open, but where was he?

He wasn't there.

That man... He'd killed Daddy...

Who was he...

She slowed, falling to her knees. She was in the middle of a street, surrounded by burnt-out shops, bits of paper and debris dancing upon the wind.

She heard all kinds of sounds.

A growl.

A screech.

And, worse of all – a hiss.

A Lisker.

She'd never seen one in person, but her dad had been sure to teach her how to recognise the sound, how to know when the threat was approaching.

She buried her face in her hands and cried.

She had nowhere to go.

How could she escape a Lisker?

How could she even hide from one?

A few more screeches prompted her to look up to the sky.

She saw them in the distance. Circling.

Had they seen her?

Of course they'd seen her.

How would they not have seen her?

"Hey!" came a voice to her right, and she abruptly turned.

She saw no one.

"In the library!"

There was what looked like it was once a library – taped up cracks in the windows and remnants of scattered, ripped paper.

The Masketes came into view.

"In here, quick!"

Without any other options, she followed the voice.

Found her way to where *he* was waiting for her.

Waiting, as he had been for a while, to take her to her new home.

Her new, perfect home.

Perfect as perfect can seem, anyway.

# CHAPTER FIFTY-NINE

A bandage around his back, he walked.

Her hand in his, trudging through the forest, as they always did.

As they had been for months.

Together.

They were with that other man, but he was gone now.

Something had happened to him.

*I'd watched it all.*

She'd tortured him. Stuck knives in his feet, his hand. Left him screaming in the garden. Walked out, slit his throat, and left the remnants for the Masketes.

It was brutal.

*It almost made me feel queasy.*

But it didn't.

*Because I've done far worse...*

And they kept walking. While it was light, they walked. When it was dark, either they built shelter, or they found somewhere to hide.

Sometimes, they came in contact with creatures, but they were good. At least, she was – he appeared to be unhelpful.

She'd hear them coming and she'd find a hiding place as quick as the flick of a knife. They'd wait it out, waiting longer than they had to, far longer.

*I'd sat and watched them far beyond when it went dark.*

Sometimes they'd fall asleep.

*And I'd still watch them then.*

They rarely, if ever, came across other survivors.

That they knew of, of course.

But a woman like this could be of great use.

He couldn't.

But they had the perfect way for getting rid of a child like that.

*We'll discard him the first chance I get.*

But her...

The difficulty would be in gaining her trust.

She didn't look the kind of person who would give trust easily. Especially after what she'd been through.

But one would have to gain it.

*And that may take time...*

But, once gained, maybe she'd be trusting enough to leave the boy alone.

That's when he could be dealt with.

*I don't know if I have that long... They may want me to be quicker...*

Well they would have to wait.

The girl stopped. Lifted his shirt. Took out a bottle of expired antiseptic she'd found at the pharmacist, the one with barely anything left.

The pharmacist where she'd heard a noise.

*But then I hid, and they had no idea.*

She applied the antiseptic to his back, and he cried out but not as much as he used to. He was growing. Maturing. Getting more used to this world.

He was still of no use, however.

He didn't seem... with it.

They needed people who were with it.

She reapplied the bandage and stood up. Smiled at him. Took his hand.

She always did that. It looked so strange. He was taller than her.

An odd pairing, really.

Couldn't be related. Not by the look of them.

So why...

They carried on walking, but they were easy to keep up with.

Out of sight.

Watching.

Waiting.

For the time to make the move.

*To introduce myself.*

And that time was almost near.

All that waiting.

Watching.

Witnessing.

I was time to make the introductions.

He had Cathryn, now it was time to acquire these two as well.

The time to step out of the shadows and appear as the saviour.

That time was arriving.

And it couldn't arrive soon enough.

BOOK THREE IS AVAILABLE NOW

# RICK WOOD



# AFTER THE LIVING HAVE LOST

# WOULD YOU LIKE TWO FREE BOOKS?

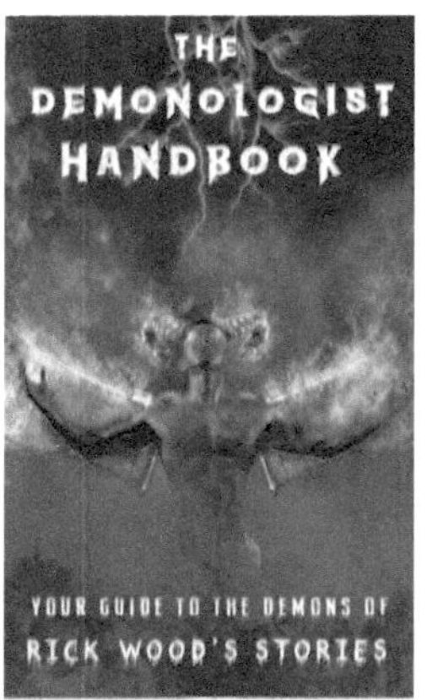



Join Rick's Reader's Group at www.
rickwoodwriter.com/sign-up

**Standalones:**

*When Liberty Dies*

*I Do Not Belong*

*Death of the Honeymoon*


**Sean Mallon:**

*Book One – The Art of Murder*

*Book Two – Redemption of the Hopeless*


**The Edward King Series:**

*Book One – I Have the Sight*

*Book Two – Descendant of Hell*

*Book Three – An Exorcist Possessed*

*Book Four – Blood of Hope*

*Book Five – The World Ends Tonight*


**Non-Fiction**

How to Write an Awesome Novel


*Thrillers published as Ed Grace:*


**The Jay Sullivan Thriller Series**

Assassin Down

Kill Them Quickly

The Bars That Hold Me

9 781838 070717